About the Author

Sarah was born in Connecticut. After earning her Bachelor's degree from Gordon College in Wenham, Massachusetts, Sarah taught for several years. Currently, she lives in Texas with her husband, John, where she is undertaking the not-so-tranquil task of raising their three sons. Learn more about Sarah here:

www.sarahhendricks.org
www.instagram.com/elvish_storybook
www.facebook.com/sarahhendricks213

Ella

Sarah Hendricks

Ella

Vanguard Press

VANGUARD PAPERBACK

© Copyright 2024
Sarah Hendricks

The right of Sarah Hendricks to be identified as author of this work has been asserted by her in accordance with the Copyright, Designs and Patents Act 1988.

All Rights Reserved

No reproduction, copy or transmission of this publication may be made without written permission.
No paragraph of this publication may be reproduced, copied or transmitted save with the written permission of the publisher, or in accordance with the provisions of the Copyright Act 1956 (as amended).

Any person who commits any unauthorised act in relation to this publication may be liable to criminal prosecution and civil claims for damages.

A CIP catalogue record for this title is available from the British Library.

ISBN 978 1 83794 072 1

This is a work of fiction. Names, characters, businesses, places, events and incidents are either the product of the author's imagination or used in a fictitious manner. Any resemblance to actual persons, living or dead, or actual events is purely coincidental.

Vanguard Press is an imprint of
Pegasus Elliot Mackenzie Publishers Ltd.
www.pegasuspublishers.com

First Published in 2024

Vanguard Press
Sheraton House Castle Park
Cambridge England

Printed & Bound in Great Britain

Dedication

To John, Noah, Ezra and Josiah

Acknowledgements

Thank you to the team at Pegasus Publishers for making my dream come true. Thank you, Erin Phillips, for your kindness in taking the time out of your own writing life to read *Ella* and give such helpful feedback. And thank you, Alissa Zavalianos, for introducing us, and for introducing me to a wonderful writing community. Thank you to my writing group, especially Phil Bryan and Aaron Wilkinson, for listening to countless chapters about elves and giving me feedback, all the while helping me hold onto my self-esteem. And thank you, Eric Beach, for inviting me to share my stories with someone other than my computer. Thank you to my mom and dad for always believing me and teaching me to believe in myself. Thank you, Noah, Ezra and Josiah, for bringing so much joy into my life, being the three best sons a mother could hope for and for believing in my writing. Thank you, John, for being the greatest husband in the whole world and supporting me in all my writing endeavours. Thank you for carving out time in our chaotic schedule for me to write. Thank you for being the person I wanted to share my heart and stories with. And thank you for tirelessly reading my work. Thank you to all of my mentors, friends and family who have encouraged me along my writing journey.

Alveland Palace District

- Groves + Gardens
- (Netherelves) NORTH MOUNTAINS
- Bactai
- East Hills
- Menatu University
- Pitchberry Forest
- Foothills
- Highland Elvish Dwellings
- Keeper's Dwelling
- Portal to Pennsylvania Cave, USA
- Rope Swing
- Grassy Knoll
- Westlands Grass
- Wildflowers
- Grassland + Wildflowers
- Town Elvish Dwellings
- Rocky Cliffs
- Faindle River
- Adviser Dwellings
- Manila's
- Far lands
- Main way
- shoppes
- Islands
- Palace
- Ocean Fjord
- Portal to Reykjavik, Iceland
- Portal to Connecticut, USA
- Coyote Desert

Part I

"Sometimes, in order to free ourselves from our self-imposed prison, we must hit rock bottom. And for that, we have life to thank."

Chapter 1

In the Alley

Friday, September 1, 1899

Ella ran across the fjord toward home. The dirt path wound its way into town. Ella felt afraid she'd cause a scene by running down Main Way, so she veered down the alley instead.

Oof. As she soared past the rear of Marilla's she ran into something solid — something solid that smelled good.

"Good evening."

Dang. Even the smell couldn't redeem this meeting. It was Oliver. She tried to swerve around him, but he sidestepped, blocking her way.

"I heard you were in town." Ella crossed her arms.

"Off to Ma and Pa's?"

"It is where I live."

"Planning to go from your mother's game group to Emil's game group?"

So what if that was the plan? If Oliver was against game group, he'd obviously never tried the tarts. "I have my elvish duties to attend to."

"So does everyone else."

Ella put her hand on the nearby fence bringing forth a daisy from a nearby flower pot. She didn't have to stand here beneath Oliver's judgment. "If you'll excuse me, I'd like to go to bed."

"Already?" Oliver raised an eyebrow.

Ella looked up into his handsome features, only barely illuminated by the alley sconces. Oliver's wavy brown hair flopped forward, creating a dangerous shadow across his face. She wasn't afraid of him, though. And she certainly didn't owe Oliver an explanation for her early bedtime. "Yes. I'm tired."

"Still jump off the rope swing?" Curiosity laced his question.

Sometimes she did. "Oh yeah, sure, Ollie. Every day."

The corner of his lip twitched into something almost resembling a smile.

That'd be a first.

Ella tried to sidestep him again, but he blocked her a second time.

She rolled her eyes and stepped the other way, but Oliver moved with her. Ella felt the familiar heat of her temper simmering in her stomach. She clenched her hands into fists and looked up into Oliver's face. The amused expression was just about enough to set her off.

"We are not kids anymore, Oliver. Let me by or I'll–"

"Or you'll what?"

Ella was not in the mood for games. Tomorrow was certain to be a difficult day. She just wanted to be in her bed where Mitsy could bring her a cup of bedtime tea and she could wallow in her misery. The last place she wanted to be was in an alley with Oliver.

She stepped once more, but this time — when Oliver blocked her — she allowed herself to knock into his hard chest. An inquisitive look furrowed his brow, and she allowed herself to enjoy the scent of his cologne for just a second. Then she calculated her three-point maneuver, kicked off her shoes and executed. First, she nudged her hip against Oliver's. Second, she wrapped her inside leg around the back of his while pinning his arm against his side. Finally, she used her free hand to simply… knock him on his ass.

The shocked expression on his face was probably the most satisfying feeling she'd had all day. Tossing her platinum ringlets so they fell behind her, she leaned in close to Oliver's ear.

"Thanks for that. It's been a while."

She left Oliver sitting in the middle of the alley and walked slowly home toward bed and tea.

"Come on Emil. Race me," Ella said the next morning.

"That wouldn't be fair to you." Emil smirked.

"Beat me then." Ella ran out the front door of the palace, her skirts skimming over the field of wild flowers. She squinted into the sun, an unusual choice for Alveland weather, considering what she knew was approaching. Ella reached out to the grass and trees, searching for the peace of its spirit, but all she felt was heaviness.

Emil waited for her to get a hearty lead, then surged past her and stopped short so she slammed against him.

"I told you."

Ella wrapped her arms around Emil, breathing in his familiar scent. He stiffened. She dared to glance at him, but he wouldn't meet her eyes. This was it. This was the moment that had been coming for weeks. She placed her hand on Emil's chest, feeling his heart and his energy. Yes, she could definitely feel it.

"Your heart is no longer yours to give, is it, Emil?"

Emil kissed Ella's forehead and tucked one of her stray locks of hair behind her ear. Then he unwrapped her hands from his waist. How could this be happening? Ella had been chosen for Prince Emil when they were wee. Her parents had always spoken of it with King Frederick and Queen Sophia.

"My parents are extremely upset," Emil's baritone voice rang with regret.

"For breaking off our engagement?" Ella asked.

Emil nodded. "Also, I did something insane."

Ella raised an eyebrow.

Emil exhaled. "I introduced them to Karina."

"You didn't." Ella's hand covered her mouth.

Emil nodded again.

"The human?"

He nodded again.

"Good luck with that," Ella giggled.

"Thanks for your support."

"I think I'm allowed to delight in your misfortune, today."

"True."

Emil nodded farewell, slid his hands into his pockets and walked back to the palace, leaving Ella alone in the field of palace wild flowers. As though they could sense her coming heartache, daisies sprouted around Ella, their faces reaching toward her. After Emil had left, Ella lay down in the flowers and began humming softly. She wove her fingers through the plants and closed her eyes. Satisfaction sank into her center as she sang fruitfulness into the earth. Plants and animals in the palace sector of Alveland owed their life cycles to her. When she sat up, she saw that the circle of daisies had sprouted fuller.

The sadness had not begun to envelop her, yet. Still, she fed her need for Alveland's energy by removing her shoes. She wandered down the abandoned afternoon streets of town toward the ocean so she could breathe in the salty air of the fjord. She dangled her legs over the side of an ocean rock and enjoyed stillness, listening to the comfort of the crashing waves.

Clumsy footsteps approached. Ella, still facing the sea, smiled, knowing immediately who they belonged to.

"Why didn't you stop me from drinking so much ale last night?" The owner of the clumsy feet plunked down ungracefully beside Ella. It was Margaret Divana Berendaily, Spirit of Fire. But Ella called her Megs.

"I tried. You wouldn't listen."

"That's no excuse. This hangover has to be your fault."

Ella giggled.

"It's not funny." Megs' raven hair fell forward over her legs as she buried her face in her knees. "Do we have to sit in the sun? It's so bright."

"You're against sunshine, now?" Ella asked.

"Only when I'm hungover."

"So, frequently?"

Megs gave her a deadpan look.

Ella sprouted to her feet and lent Megs a hand.

"Woah, woah, woah," Megs said. "What's wrong?"

"What do you mean?"

Megs motioned to the semicircle of wild flowers crowding around Ella's rock. "Alveland is comforting you. Why?"

Ella sighed. She didn't want to talk about her break-up. She wanted to avoid the topic for as long as possible.

"Do I know why?"

Ella nodded.

"That fool."

"He's not a fool, he's the Prince. I'll tell you about it on our way to the Keeper's."

"Not the Keeper's," whined Megs.

"I'm not dealing with you hungover all day."

"I'll just mix up a remedy in my shop later." Megs dragged her feet as Ella pulled her down the hill, away from the fjord.

The Keeper's house was built into the side of the foothill mountains. Ella noticed blue smoke curling out of the chimney before knocking on the door.

The door opened a crack and Ella could see the Keeper's eye peek out at them.

"Best Day, Miss Ella. Do come in," he said. "At your service."

He had called her by her common title. How did he already know about her break-up with the Prince?

"It is my job to know the things of Alveland," the Keeper answered her unasked question.

"Alveland, yes, but not the business of every elf in Alveland," Ella said.

"I suggest that it is all one and the same," the Keeper said.

"Megs has a hangover," Ella said.

The old elf shuffled into his closet of a kitchen and began removing bottles and vials.

"Other than the alcohol consequences, how fares the day?"

Stepping over piles of books and papers, Ella made her way into the Keeper's kitchen and recounted the events of her morning. She glanced at the bowed bookshelves which lined the walls of the Keeper's house, holding all the records of Alveland both from him and from all the Keepers before.

"Hm." The Keeper kept his expression neutral as he mixed and poured.

Ella guessed that Megs appreciated the dim lighting in the house. At least elves didn't have to worry about alcohol related liver damage the way humans do. A sour tummy and a headache were about as bad as it got, however unpleasant.

When the remedy was prepared, the Keeper delivered it to the creaky table nestled in the breakfast nook. The three of them sat around it. Megs stared at the drink.

"Down it goes," Ella said.

Megs glowered at her encouragement, and reluctantly sipped. Ella laughed as Megs shivered from the bitter liquid. Ella knew that feeling.

"Who inspired this display of alcohol consumption?" Ella asked.

Megs grunted, "Chamden."

Ella raised an eyebrow.

"You know he's handsome," Megs said. "We just kept drinking and dancing and dancing and drinking."

Ella laughed.

"Not so loud," Megs said.

"Hunters are back," the Keeper said.

"I heard." Megs massaged her temples.

"Even Oliver."

Ella knew that already.

"Does that mean…" Ella was afraid to finish her question.

The Keeper nodded.

"How long do you think we have?" Ella asked.

"Last time it was less than two days," the Keeper said.

"Hopefully long enough for one of them to take me out for dinner," Megs said.

"Seriously?" Ella asked.

"They have to eat," Megs said.

Ella rolled her eyes.

"I better go check on ShaSha." Ella stood up and looked out the tiny window of the kitchen. "Feeling better?" She turned to Megs.

Megs took the last drink of her remedy and shook her head as it slid down. "Yeesh. That stuff works, but it's terrible."

The Keeper chuckled and led the two out the front door.

"Thank you," said Ella.

"It is always a pleasure." Smile lines creased the Keeper's face.

Megs hugged Ella. "Thank you for taking care of me."

"I always will," Ella said. Megs seemed more like a sister than a friend at this point. Which is extra special for an elf, because most don't have siblings. "Make good choices. I'm going to ShaSha."

―――

ShaSha was catching bugs outside her bedroom window when she returned to her house. Ella whistled and the chameleon climbed onto her hand, allowing her to bring him inside.

"Best stay inside for a few days, ShaSha," she said.

She felt the chameleon's wiggly energy along his spine. Though chameleons move quite slowly, their energy is quick, radiating in little waves. She placed him on the skirts of her pink gown and delighted in watching him change color.

"Not very manly of you," Ella giggled.

"Did you find ShaSha?" *Pop*. Megs' sound message came into her room with its customary '*pop*'.

"He's fine," *Pop*, said Ella. "He was catching bugs in our sycamore." *Pop*.

A tear hit Ella's dress. ShaSha turned an eye to look directly at Ella.

"I'm not going to be the Princess anymore," Ella whispered.

The sadness was coming.

Chapter 2

Jandotter's Cafe

Sunday, September 3, 1899

Oliver poured himself a cup of coffee. He had expected to go drinking at Marilla's, which he did. He had expected to meet Kaitlin there, which he did. He had expected to go six rounds on top in the Glima pit, which he did. He had expected that he and Kaitlin would drink too much, and that they would then go back to his place, which he did. But he had not expected to find himself on his ass in the alley behind Marilla's.

It was time to get to his assembly. He had less than an hour before the Hunters' Summit, which would give him just enough time to grab breakfast on the way. The Hunters needed to figure out what in the hell to do with the Shadow. How could it have come to the Palace Province? Then again, how could it not. It sought out power and energy, which the Palace Province had in abundance. But first breakfast. He shouldered his knapsack, downed the last of his coffee and left his dwelling for the day. The Palace Province had put him up in one of their council dwellings. They were small and on the outskirts, of course, but still a convenient walk to the palace.

It had been a good five years since he had passed through the Palace Province, but he was happy to see Jandotter's Cafe still open for breakfast. The lamp in the window was a beacon for him in the dim dawn light. A bell jangled as he entered.

"Be still my heart. Oliver Agnarsson Belwin, Spirit of the Ocean, is in my cafe."

Oliver nodded in response to Jill's outburst.

"Want your usual?"

"You remember my usual?"

Jill smirked, ducked into the kitchen and re-emerged with two poached eggs on toast with a side of skyr and berries. A small side plate held his grilled herring.

Oliver inhaled the aroma deeply and let out an audible sigh.

He picked up his fork to start on his breakfast when the doorbell jangled again. This time, though, the door smashed against the wall. Oliver grabbed his wolf cane. A lad-elf charged into the room, looking over his shoulder. Great. Just what every peaceful morning needed: a kid.

"Gunnar do not tell me that you have run away from your nanny again," Jill said.

Gunnar's eyes narrowed. "Don't need a nanny."

He picked a table far from the window, obviously hoping not to be seen.

Oliver knew that this must have been what he looked like as a youth. He used to ditch his nanny, too.

"Did your ma feed you, at least, before sending you off on all this disobedience?" Jill asked.

The boy looked hungrily at Oliver's breakfast.

Oliver looked at his timepiece and rolled his eyes. Despite the time, he placed his breakfast in front of the boy. Devin used to do the same thing for him when he sneaked into Marilla's to watch Glima.

"Wow. You're Oliver Agnarsson, Spirit of the Ocean."

Oliver knew that.

"Thanks, sir," Gunnar said.

Oliver nodded.

Jill winked at him and ducked back in the kitchen to fetch another round of breakfast for Oliver. Oliver took his timepiece from his pants pocket and lay it on the table. He hoped delaying breakfast wouldn't make him late to the summit.

Oliver watched as Gunnar took a cerulean-furred Slow Loris out of his cloak hood. The kid broke up some of his fish and set them out on the table for it. The way Gunnar kept looking up from breakfast to check the window made Oliver nervous.

Checking his timepiece once more, Oliver stuffed in one more bite of breakfast, left enough coins on the table to cover two breakfasts and quit the cafe. On his way out the door he collided with a flustered female elf who appeared to be missing someone.

Oliver looked over his shoulder at the woman and shuddered. With the Spirits as his witness, he would never have wees.

Chapter 3

Brittany

Sunday, September 3, 1899

Ella wrapped herself in her fuzziest, pink elvish robe, stuck her feet inside of her warmest dwelling slippers and scuffed her way to breakfast.

"Morning Miss Ella," said Mitsy, as she entered the dining hall. "Here's your coffee. Chef Devan will have your breakfast out in just a minute."

"There's my baby."

Ella bristled at the sound of her mother's fussing voice. The Ella-fussing always seemed like a contradiction to Maria Marina's strong and intelligent countenance.

"Missed you yesterday, Princess." Because of how elves age, Maria Andevi Marina, Spirit of Wind, did not look more than a few years older than her daughter. Ella was one hundred and twenty-eight years old, which is about seventeen in human years. Maria and Ella shared the same blonde hair, though Ella's had the bounciest of curls, while her mother's was straight as an elf-cut brick.

"Not a Princess anymore," said Ella.

Mrs Marina sighed.

"It's fine."

"I still think you should let your father talk to King Frederick."

"No, Ma." Ella could not think of anything more humiliating than having her dad talk to Emil's father about their broken engagement. She just wanted to forget about yesterday's break-up. It was over, and she wanted to move on. Her brain needed a good distraction from Emil, Princess-ships, weddings, etc.

"We made an arrangement with King Frederick and Queen Sophia, and it should be honored." Foam started to form in the corner of her mother's mouth as she spoke.

"I don't want to marry Emil any more, Ma. Not when he loves someone else."

Tears misted Maria's eyes. She looked like she was about to break down about it.

"Can we just eat?"

"Morning." Her father, Argon Darion Marina, Spirit of Earthen Cliffs, entered the dining hall.

"Hi Pa."

"Ella Manweli Marina, Spirit of Flower, is that you?"

Ella rolled her eyes. "Yes, Pa, it's me."

"Can I finally have your blessing to speak with our King on your behalf? I think it's time we put all this behind us. Sort out this engagement."

"No, Pa. I mean it." Then she added, "Or Emil."

Her father looked at her disapprovingly.

"Oliver's back with the Hunters," Maria said to her husband. "Maybe he can talk some sense into Emil."

"He'd have to have some sense, first," said Ella. She thought of their childish interaction behind the alley last night and rolled her eyes. If there was one thing Oliver's already difficult personality didn't need, it was buckets of fame.

She looked up into her parents' worried eyes. They were waiting for her to crumble. Not that it hadn't happened before.

"You okay, Ellie-Boo?" her mother finally asked.

"Fine," Ella said.

"Maybe a walk into town would do you some good."

"Maybe." As much as she didn't want to agree with her mother, she could use a distraction, and she always liked town.

"I'll send Mitsy up to redo your make-up and plait your hair after breakfast."

"What's wrong with my make-up and hair?" Ella said.

"You never know who you might meet."

"Who will I meet?"

Her mother gave her a knowing look.

"I'm not patrolling for lad-elves. Emil and I just broke up."

You had a Prince and a future and now you have neither.

Ella named the derogatory voice in her mind Brittany. Ella wished it was easier to argue with Brittany. She had to get out of the dining room because Brittany and her mother, together, were too much.

"You know what? That will be great, Mom. Send Mitsy up and I'll get dressed." She pinched the bridge of her nose to keep away the headache she called her mom-throb and escaped to her room.

Ella's elvish slippers crunched beneath her as she approached town. Mitsy had helped her dress in a long linen elf dress in lavender. She had braided Ella's hair into a crown all around her head, and curled wispy tendrils to frame her face and neck. When Mitsy had finished her hair and make-up, Ella had trodden in her gardens and sang to them. She sang to her apple orchard and procured an apple for a snack. When she crossed the Fainde River, she dallied below the bridge and dipped her feet in the cool, rushing ripples. Eventually, she submerged her legs far enough that she could feel the smooth rocks in the riverbed.

Next, Ella window-shopped along Main Way. She turned down Vander Lane. It was darker, and contained older buildings full of small shops. The end shop was Megs', Megs' Emporium of Eclectic Paraphernalia and Mixes. A bell rang as she opened the door and a strong scent of apple and vanilla wafted out.

"Make yourself at home. Be with you soon," Megs hollered from the back room.

Ella ran her gaze across the many glass shelves surrounding Megs' shop. Pots and bowls of every color and shape lay on display. Across the back wall were canisters of labeled herbs and other natural materials that Megs used in her mixes. Ella didn't make many mixes, but many elves used herbs and plants in home recipes and remedies. Some of them required magic and some of them didn't.

"How can I help… oh, it's you." Megs emerged from behind the dividing curtain. "Need anything?"

Ella shook her head.

"Have a mix." Megs wiped the granite countertop then clanged a large shot glass down in front of Ella. She poured in a green liquid from the cooler. Ella watched as she skillfully crushed some herbs in a clay pot. When she added them to the liquid, a small puff of smoke erupted from the glass.

"I'm not drinking an exploding beverage," Ella said.

"It's just the carbonation," Megs said.

"What will it do to me?" Ella looked at her quizzically.

"It's a pick-me-up. Nothing weird, I promise."

Though Megs was a free spirit, Ella trusted her with her life, so she took a sip. The carbonation tickled her nose. To her surprise, she did not feel weird at all. In fact, she felt pretty good.

"How's town?" Megs asked.

"Good to be out."

Ella could tell that her friend wanted to ask about her break-up. She didn't want to talk about it.

"How are... other things?" Megs asked. Ella told her about her parents and ShaSha, the river and town. She felt better staying with lighter subjects.

"I've got an order to get together for Jill Jandotter. Want to come in the back with me?" Megs asked.

"I think I'll go for a walk. Thanks for the mix." The little bell on the door rang again as Ella quit the building and returned to Main Way.

The sconce outside her favorite shop flickered invitingly. Aerilaya Brandydottr, Spirit of Flight, owned Aerilaya's. Ella noticed Aerilaya's dimple appear as she spoke with a mother and daughter in her shop. Ella spotted a pink silk dress with a corset hanging on display. She couldn't stop herself from going to see it. She'd just look at it. Maybe touch it. It felt soft and cool against her fair skin. She reached into her side pouch and fingered the money her mother had given her.

You still take money from your mother, Brittany reminded her.

She resented that fact. But when was she supposed to have gotten a job? Certainly not when she was attending Lady Lessons. And why would she have ever needed a career when — up until yesterday — she was going to be a Princess?

Her resentment did not change the fact the dress was gorgeous — special. She swallowed her pride and asked Aerilaya to wrap it up for her.

"This is my favorite," Aerilaya skillfully folded the dress. "A good pick-me-up for any lady-elf."

Ella noticed Aerilaya's specific language which avoided the word 'princess'. Everyone in Alveland already seemed to know that she and Emil had broken up, and that she could use a pick-me-up. "Plans for today?" Ella asked.

Aerilaya leaned her elbows on the counter. Her soft curls formed a halo around her head before falling down her back. "Probably go see the fights." She shrugged. "Should be good with the Hunters in town."

Ella agreed. When she left the shop, her stomach grumbled, so she headed toward Marilla's to get lunch. As soon as she entered the dimly lit bar, however, she wished she could dash out. But it was too late. She had already been spotted by Emil, Oliver and a plain looking woman who could only be Emil's human girlfriend, Karina.

Emil waved her over to the bar. Her fists clenched at her sides as her stomach clenched within her. Would this human become Princess of Alveland? Surely not. She wasn't even an elf. How could someone who wasn't an elf rule Alveland? Good manners prevented her from avoiding Emil. He stood as she approached the table.

"Ella, this is Karina. Karina, Ella."

Karina stood. Ella's breath caught in her chest, but she brought her right fist across herself and bowed. Karina returned the honor. She was cute, Ella would admit that. Lovely, even, for a human.

"Let me buy you lunch. You can join us," Emil said to Ella.

"Unfortunately, I have to take my lunch to go." Ella had addressed the Prince and honored Karina. She was under no obligation to stay.

She waved to Bear Kiepersol, Spirit of Islands, as he passed by with his towel.

"Lady Ella." Bear bowed low.

"You don't have to do that, any more," Ella whispered so only Bear could hear.

He looked uncomfortably past her at Emil and then back at her. "I will always bow to your elvish beauty, Miss Ella." He whispered, too.

Could this moment be any more awkward? Brittany asked.

Ella did feel unworthy of Bear's honor.

"What can I get you?" Bear asked.

"Just a fish mix sandwich." It was easier to talk about sandwiches than Emil.

"That it?"

"Maybe some potatoes," Ella said. Then she added, "To go, please."

"Right away." Bear slung his towel over his pudgy shoulder and went into the kitchen. How had Bear ended up with pudge? All the other elves she knew were thin and sleek. Some elves say his father was a troll. He came from the mountains, so no one knew his parents. Maybe he was. Although, Bear seemed much too kind-hearted to have any troll in him.

Bear slid an ale to her along the pine wood bar to enjoy while she waited. She climbed onto the stool next to

Oliver. As she sat down, she caught sight of a table of young lass-elves who were whispering and giggling and pointing at Oliver. How subtle of them.

"Ella," Oliver said.

"Oliver." Ella looked away and rolled her eyes. Her food could not come fast enough.

"Will you be back for the fights?" Bear placed her brown bag of food in front of her at the bar.

"Not sure."

"Should be interesting." Bear motioned with his head toward Oliver. "Some out-of-towners are fighting."

Definitely not then. "Maybe. Thanks for the food."

Chapter 4

Marilla's

Sunday, September 3, 1899

"Come o-on." Megs was drawing out single syllable words as she whined. Ella had returned her feet to her dwelling slippers, pulled out her braid and hidden under her covers in order to distract herself from her afternoon. She had gone to town in order to distract herself from Emil which had been an epic failure. She had run into both him and his new love. Yes, Ella was hiding under the comfort of her bedcovers when Megs stopped by on her way home from town.

"Absolutely not," Ella said. She just wanted to stay home and wallow.

"You have to," Megs said.

"Why?"

"Because I want you to."

Ella gave her a deadpan look.

"I didn't hear a 'no', that time."

"Something tells me this is not a good idea," Ella said.

"When have I ever led you astray?" Even Megs couldn't get through that sentence with a straight face.

"How about the time we played pirates as wee ones?" Ella said.

"Would you still hold that against me?" Megs asked.

"We almost died."

"Small detail."

"Troll's lair before Lady Lesson tea?"

"Just a little mud. Nothing dangerous."

"My mother wanted to kill me."

"But she didn't."

Ella rolled her eyes. She had a perfectly quiet evening planned that involved her cozy bedroom, hot tea from Mitsy and a visit with ShaSha. And of course, her overwhelming sadness. Now, somehow, Megs had convinced her to attend the fights at Marilla's. Ella rang for Mitsy to ask her about steaming her new dress instead of bringing her tea.

"By the Spirits, it's beautiful, Miss Ella." The corners of Mitsy's eyes crinkled as she rubbed the silk of the new dress between her fingers. "A fine choice."

Ella found comfort in Mitsy's affirmation. The lady's maid had swept her brown hair into a twist. Gray highlights framed her face.

"What time are you meeting Miss Margaret? You get out your petticoats and I'll steam this for you. She took the dress with her as she hurried out of the room.

Ella boarded her rolling closet ladder and extracted three petticoats. She laid them out on the bed and drew a hot bath for herself. She peered out of the bathroom at the petticoats as the tub filled. Royal elves were required to wear several petticoats. Royal elves like Princesses. Did she really need all those petticoats anymore? She shrugged. She was used to it. She'd just wear them anyways.

Mitsy returned with a freshly steamed dress. She applied some light blush to Ella's cheeks in order to bring out her rosy complexion, then set her long hair in rollers. The rollers made Ella's already-curly, waist-length hair smooth and bouncy. Last, Ella opened her jewelry box in order to accessorize. She chose a rose gold choker set with a giant pink topaz which would match well with her dress.

You look like a Princess. You act like a Princess. And you were engaged to the Prince. So how is it possible that you aren't going to be a Princess? That was Brittany, again.

Thank you, Brittany.

As her pink evening slippers crunched along the rocks and seashells beneath her feet, Ella breathed in glorious, salty sea air that wafted in from the harbor. Ella heard the sound of folk music with her elvish ears before she saw the pointed roof and glowing sconces of Marilla's. It was nearly ten o'clock. Marilla's would just start to come alive as the night's fight tournament approached.

She creaked open the thick, front door and the sound of many conversations, jeers and cheers met her ears. She scanned the room for Megs who, of course, was flirting at the bar. Probably with one of the Hunters. Megs tossed her hair and rested her hand on the stranger's arm. Oh Megs. Ella wove through the crowd toward her. When she saw Emil and Karina sitting a little ways down the bar, her stomach clenched again, as it had earlier in the afternoon. Karina had her hood up — probably trying not to draw attention to the fact that she was a human and wildly out of place in Alveland. Emil was brave to bring her. Then again, Emil had always pushed limits. Why had she fallen in love with Emil? It wasn't a requirement for their arranged marriage. She would just have to figure out a way to get over that. She longed for the soothing energy of Alveland. She needed more daisies. Alveland was farther away through the wooden floors of Marilla's.

"Woah." Ella was launched from her sadness by Megs' embrace of greeting. Megs wore a drop-dead dress, black to match her hair, and berry red lip paint. Her eyes were thickly lined and Ella thought she looked wonderful.

"Here." Megs pulled a long leather cord with a charm out of her bag. She tied it around Ella's neck.

"What's this?" Ella lifted the charm which hung between her breasts. She sucked in her breath. It was a colorful mini of the fern flower.

"You're my nomination," Megs said. "What's it that I always say?"

"Courage, adventure, luck midst strife, keeps a good life in Alveland," both girls said together. Ella knew Megs' life motto by heart.

"You're going to make it," Megs whispered.

Ella felt the empty spot on her finger where her engagement ring used to sit. Thinking about her lost life as a Princess and her lost love, Ella didn't always believe she was going to make it. She was thankful for her braided hair, her new dress and her rosy make-up from Mitsy. The get-up hid her misery well. And she was thankful that Megs was with her, not asking her to talk about Emil.

Cheers from the Glima pit drew Ella's attention. She and Megs leaned over the balcony and looked into the basement and into the Glima pit. Oliver was standing in the center of the pit, and his damp hair stuck to his forehead.

"Oliver's just won the first round of the night's victor match. He's fighting Benjamin," Megs said.

Ella came to Marilla's often enough to know that Benjamin was one of the town's regular victors. He was still young — a fairly new fighter who had hung around Marilla's long before he was old enough to fight. Just like Oliver.

"I'll take one of those to go." Megs was watching Oliver towel off his very muscular body.

"You've said that before."

"Have I?"

Ella smirked.

Megs shrugged.

"What about your new friend at the bar?"

"He's cute, too."

Ella looked back at Oliver. He had turned so his muscular back was facing them. Despite her unending irritation with him, Ella could not argue with Megs about Oliver's physical perfection.

Ella enjoyed watching the last two rounds of the fighting. Excitement radiated through her muscles as she watched. Benjamin won the middle round, throwing Oliver to the ground with an under the throat takedown. But Oliver won the final round with an over the shoulder takedown.

Somber faced, he raised a fist in the air to acknowledge the adoring cheers. The twittering energy from the crowd radiated over the banister toward Oliver. The Palace Province of Alveland truly admired him. Probably even more for his Hunting than Glima. Ella knew he could feel their gratefulness. He crossed his chest with his right fist and bowed to them. Then, he wove his way through a crowd of fawning young women to the bar privy where he would have a minute of peace to clean himself.

"How are you, Miss Quiet?" Megs nudged Ella's shoulder. They turned away from the fights and leaned their backs against the banister. Ella drained the last of her ale. Megs motioned to Bear for a round of shots.

"It's going to be difficult at first. But you'll feel like yourself again," Megs said.

"I was never myself," Ella said. She looked over at Emil and felt her heart squeeze. Megs would never understand. Megs had always known who she was and fought her way to get there. It was different for Ella. She was the daughter of two Palace Advisors. She had been groomed for the position of the Princess of Alveland. Now she was just Ella — someone she was yet to know. She pulled at the skirt of her dress. "Probably shouldn't buy clothes like this anymore."

"Anyone deserves a pretty dress," Megs said. "Although, you could take it off and watch Bear have a heart attack. And probably half the guys in the bar."

Ella gave her a deadpan look.

"Have I mentioned that Emil is a fool?" Megs asked.

"Yes," Ella said.

"Now we need to find you someone new." Megs scanned the room.

"You're going to find me a new husband in this room?"

"Heavens, no. I'm going to find you a dance partner."

Ella pinched the bridge of her nose. "I'm getting my Margaret headache."

"Fine. Cease fire."

"Thank you."

"We'll figure it out." Megs wrapped her arms around Ella.

Megs disappeared for a moment then returned. She led Ella onto the dance floor as though she were a stubborn toddler.

The musicians began a jig. Megs shoved Ella into Bear's arms.

Ella looked back at Megs.

Megs gave her a deadpan look. "See? I'm not evil."

"You are evil, just not at this particular moment."

Bear extended his hand to Ella.

Ella placed her hand in his and they danced. It seemed that it was still possible to have fun, even after a royally broken engagement.

It was one o'clock in the morning when Ella and Megs emerged from Marilla's. The cool air was pleasant and the silence even more so. Ella sucked in a breath of fresh ocean air and relished in having her feet back on bare ground. Ella enjoyed the rare sight of seeing an owl fly across the full moon. A treat from Alveland, to be sure. Every dancing muscle was tired and her eyes felt droopy. She was grateful for the happy distractions of Marilla's and could not wait to snuggle deep in her bed covers and sleep a long, rejuvenating sleep.

Then she felt a chill. It was colder than the night air. More than an ocean breeze. Megs gripped her arm.

"What's that?" she whispered.

Ella grabbed Megs' hand and the two ladies scanned the darkness for some sign of what could be out there. Goosebumps prickled the back of Ella's neck.

"To your dwellings or in the bar!" Three Hunters burst from Marilla's. "Charm your homes. Stay hidden."

"You're coming with me," Megs said. "My dwelling is closer." Megs' dwelling was in the same neighborhood as Marilla's.

"I have to get ShaSha."

"He'll be fine. You put him in."

"I have to make sure. Sometimes Mitsy opens the windows." Ella embraced her friend. "You go." Megs turned the other way. Ella ran toward the Fainde River Bridge.

The cold did not seem to be worsening. She could feel her heartbeat as she approached the bridge's triple arches. Footsteps approached. Fearful of even more danger, she glanced over her shoulder to see Oliver.

"What are you doing?" Oliver said.

"I have to get ShaSha."

"You can't."

Was he really trying to boss her around at a time like this? She ignored him, crossed the bridge and turned toward her dwelling in the small patch of Advisor dwellings.

"Oh no." Ella stopped suddenly. Her neighborhood was engulfed in blackness, no longer visible.

"Quickly. To the palace." Oliver's hand closed around her wrist and led her away. As they ran down the walk toward the palace, blackness slithered down the palace's buttery stones. Ella could no longer see their conical turrets.

"Come on." Oliver yanked her through the gardens toward the wall which ran next to the palace.

Ella knew where he was taking her.

Chapter 5

The Shadow

Sunday, September 3, 1899

Oliver loved Glima. Plain and simple. Pushing his muscles to their limit was satisfying. Glima was fast. He had learned when he was way too young by sneaking into fights as a wee one. Then he practiced with his friends. Now, it helped him get out his aggression. Plus, he was damn good at it. And being good at Glima kept him plenty busy with the lady-elves. Fighting came like second nature. Maybe that's why he was so good at Hunting, too. Despite the contempt he had felt for the career as a child, he had grown into Alveland's best Hunter.

Between his keen elvish vision and the flame he had created in his hand, he could see the Shadow, clearly climbing down the walls of the palace. His training kicked in. He zeroed in on the best chance of survival for himself and Ella. First, he soaked up power from Alveland's energy and transferred it to Ella so that she could keep up with him.

The Shadow had completely engulfed the palace and was still spreading. Oliver could feel the chill. Ella's fair skin was turning blue and her teeth chattered uncontrollably. He had to get himself and Ella through this doorway, but it meant trapping themselves against the wall. There were mere yards between them and the Shadow.

"Keep to the wall," Oliver said to Ella.

A wave of dread and nausea heaved his body. Inches to go. Ella sank to her knees and threw up. Oliver reluctantly let go of her arm for just a moment in order to yank open a heavy, wooden door, tucked behind the ivy on the stone wall.

Oliver helped Ella to her feet and the two forced their way through the door.

The Shadow had covered half the door. Oliver knew he had to get it closed before it reached them. He gave it a pull, but it stuck fast.

The wobbly edge of the Shadow stretched inside the door frame.

Oliver plunged his hand inside it and gave the door another yank. It slid part way closed.

Ella grabbed onto the inner door handle too. They both pulled, yelled and exerted a small amount of elvish energy and the door finally slid solidly closed. Both elves lit fires in the palms of their hands. A small piece of the Shadow had followed them. It looked like a little puff of black paint, swirling at their feet. Oliver exerted another burst of energy, and the swirl dissipated.

"Can it get in?" Ella asked.

"Don't know. I doubt it's interested."

Ella inched away from the door.

"Let's pass through the portal, just to be sure."

Oliver and Ella needed to travel to the end of the tunnel. Oliver handed down the torches tucked away in their holders. He used the flame in his hand to light his own. The two shuffled through the dirty tunnel until they reached the matching door on the other side. The cool, cast-iron door handle creaked as Ella clicked it and pulled it open. This door was much less impeded by land than the one to Alveland. Oliver never minded the human realm. He and Emil had used it as a primary location for their boyhood mischief.

"I never liked Mannland," Ella said. "I only ever got called here by Emil when he was in trouble."

Oliver could not argue that there had been plenty of trouble.

When they crossed the threshold of the next door, Oliver felt the familiar puff of wind across his face and the gentle burst of pressure in his ears as he entered the human realm. As he and Ella travelled along the tunnel and into Mannland, he calculated data in his mind. It had been one a.m. when he left Marilla's, five past one when the Shadow arrived. The Shadow was moving about twelve inches per minute. Shadow traveling east by south-east. Affected areas included palace, town dwellings, Advisor dwellings. It probably traveled east of Marilla's and would be out to sea in two hours. Longer if it slowed. It could also reach the mountains if it changed directions. The Palace Province population housed about one thousand elves. Oliver was hoping for less than one percent taken. There were five province Hunters and twenty traveling Hunters, including himself and his father. There would probably be about a months' work of regrowth and restoration. He'd be out on assignment again, or reassigned here, depending on if the Shadow returned or if he was called to retrieval. He was never called to retrieval, though.

"Where are we going?" Ella asked.

"Might as well grab a pint." Oliver had immediately begun heading to town.

"You're grabbing a pint? Now?"

"I saved you. I did my job. We can't get back in yet. We have to wait. We can either stand here and stare at each other, or grab a pint." Oliver started walking again. He could not stand and stare at Ella. It was difficult enough to have her looking down on him from the balcony during Glima.

"I don't think I'm quite the charge that I used to be," Ella said. "I'm no longer royal."

For a moment, Oliver remembered the last time he saved Ella. Last time was definitely worse. Ella had been so close to death, although, this time involved the Shadow, so maybe they had both been close to death. Last time there was so much blood, though, that it was surely worse. It was definitely time for a pint.

"Do you read, Crandy?" *Pop*. Oliver sent a sound message to his partner as they crossed the landscape into the human town.

"Read you." *Pop*. Crandy was out of breath.

"Status." *Pop*.

"Shadow's moved south to the palace. Taking a census of the path. None missing so far."

"Palace is still compromised?" *Pop*.

"Yes. Where are you?" *Pop*.

"Mannland. We were approaching the palace when the Shadow arrived. Exited a portal." *Pop*.

"Mannland?" *Pop*. "Stay safe."

"Tell me when the palace is clear. Census report: Ella Marina, Spirit of the Flower is safe. She is in Mannland with me."

The town center finally came into view. John Gregor's Old Pub was still there, where it had always been — a beacon of human fellowship on Main Street. Oliver disguised the points at the end of his ears with a charm. He hoped the palace would be clear soon. There was much to do. His body tensed with the anticipation of it all. He felt the heaviness from being without Alveland's energy. It would be good to get back. He glanced at Ella out of the corner of his eye. But in the meantime, that pint.

Chapter 6

Dagur

Sunday, September 3, 1899

Ella expected a revelation when she entered the human realm again, but there was none. Instead, she simply saw a damp expanse of land. It was beautiful, to be sure, but not as lovely as Alveland. An early autumn snow was falling. Ella reached for the earth's energy but felt very little. She became depressed, missing the vibrant pulse that beat through Alveland. Why does Emil like this place so much?

It had been years since she had been through this door, yet she remembered the way to the village — along the seashore cliffs, across a farm and then onto the village. But Oliver didn't take her that way. He took a shortcut in the opposite direction which led them right into the center of the town.

The town now looked more like a city. Ella recognized the cathedral from before, but now there were several new buildings which lit up the night with their chandeliers and sconces. A quaint college slept in the center of town, behind the open businesses. Oliver led them to John Gregor's Old Pub.

Ella's heart beat loudly in her ears. She was in Mannland — the human realm. There were troubling rumors about humans. Ella hoped they were just rumors, anyway.

"Do you think we'll be safe?" Ella asked.

"Safer than in the Palace Province," Oliver said.

That was true. Ella swiped the points off her ears with her magic as Oliver had done, thus making sure the Hidden Folk stayed hidden. John Gregor's smelled like cinnamon and whiskey-stained wood. Ella followed Oliver to the bar. The tables packed with friends and the glowey lanterns reminded her of Marilla's.

Oliver ordered them both blueberry ales. The bartender had a lot of bushy hair on his head and face. Ella could tell that he had tried, unsuccessfully, to tame it with wax. Still, looking past his wild hair, Ella thought he had friendly eyes.

Before long, a blonde woman in a corset dress took the seat on the other side of Oliver. He rudely turned away from Ella and began flirting. How could he abandon her at a time like this? Ella's home had just been attacked and now she felt exposed in the human realm.

"What are you doing?" Ella whispered.

"Perusing the menu," Oliver whispered back.

Ella rolled her eyes. He never did have trouble attracting distractions for himself of the female variety, even before he was Alveland's most famous Hunter. She swirled the berries floating in her ale. At least with Oliver distracted she could relax a little from her embarrassment. She couldn't believe that he had saved her life again. Surely this time she would have been able to save herself, right? Ella, struggling to relax without the help of Alveland, reminded herself to breathe.

"Two shots of vodka and whatever the lady's having." Ella discovered that she had attracted her own blond human. This was to be expected because of radiant elvish beauty.

"Th-thank you," she stammered.

A random guy had never bought her a drink before. Ella didn't know how to handle the situation, which did nothing to help her stress level. Emil and Bear were the only ones who bought her drinks at Marilla's. She noticed that this human had piercing, blue eyes. Ella thought he was extremely handsome — and not just for a human. She felt her cheeks grow hot.

"Dagur." He introduced himself.

"Ella."

They exchanged pleasantries while Oliver leaned close to his Blondie.

"Dae!" A plump older woman wrapped Dagur in a hug. "Thank you for helping me with all those repairs at me house. I'd never be able to do it meself. And Ernie, with his ankle swelled up. We would have been leaky and frozen." The Icelandic language sat jolly and high in the palate, much like the elvish language.

"A pleasure." Ella saw a dimple appear on his face as he smiled kindly at the old woman. Ella's stomach fluttered.

"A neighbor to my pa." Dagur turned his attention back to Ella.

Ella nodded. Whether because he was so handsome or so human, Dagur had her feeling shy.

"Dae!" Before she could find her voice, another adoring female voice cut through the crowd. A young girl — much too young to be in a bar in the middle of the night — with bouncy brown curls flew at Dagur and wrapped him in a hug.

"Bitsy, what are you doing here?"

"Sissy and Jimmy said we could pop in for a quick one. On our way back into town, now."

"You should be in bed. Are you asleep on your feet?"

"Not even a little. Woke up as we crossed the mountains in the carriage. Can we two hand jig? The band is just starting one. Me ma's been teaching me."

"My kid sister-in-law," Dagur explained.

Ella covered a smile with her hand.

Dagur theatrically bowed to Bitsy and escorted her to the dance floor in the back of the room by the musicians. Ella got to watch the dance floor from her barstool. She watched Dagur lead his niece in steps. She mostly stood on his shoes. Ella also caught sight of Oliver who was dancing with his Blondie.

When Dagur returned, his demeanor had darkened. Bitsy was with her parents on the other side of the bar and a well-dressed gentleman now held Dagur's attention. She only caught bits and pieces of their hushed conversation.

"...shouldn't be in the position to rule anyone."

"Neither should yours."

"...will have a chance to prove it. If I have anything to do with it."

"...to be careful."

"Apologies." Dagur finally returned to the bar.

His dark demeanor with his friend reminded Ella of the Shadow in Alveland and she shivered. Dagur offered Ella his coat. Ella found him funny and charming. After conversing with him for hardly any time at all, her cheeks hurt from smiling. Ella finally began to relax. Dagur sat close enough that Ella could take in his scent. He smelled like cinnamon and vodka. Or maybe that was the bar. Whatever it was, it smelled good. The strong mixture made her head feel fuzzy and she forgot about the Shadow. Which is why it was so surprising when Oliver appeared beside her.

"Gotta go," Oliver said.

Of course, they would have to leave now. She wasn't ready to leave Dagur, yet. Ella reminded herself that she could barely feel the earth's energy in Mannland. Returning would mean that she would get to return to the energy of Alveland. She could feel loads of antsy energy rippling off Oliver.

"Save me a dance next time, love." Dagur pressed Ella's hand.

Humans were more difficult to read than elves, but Ella could read the jealousy all over Dagur's face as he stared down Oliver, and she tried to think of something to assure him of her affections.

"So sorry I've got to go with... with my brother."

Oliver rolled his eyes.

Ella and Oliver tied their overcloaks and returned to the portal.

"I'll go in first." Oliver opened the door to the tunnel, pushed through the portal, lit his torch and shone it around inside. "The tunnel is clear."

Ella followed close behind. She needed to get home as soon as possible. She needed to check on her parents and ShaSha. Hopefully Megs had gotten to her dwelling in time.

Once through the tunnel and beyond the Alveland door, Ella could feel the devastation. Her Alveland was in pain. She felt the once lush grass, dry and brittle beneath her feet. Her torchlight and elvish vision revealed shriveled garden plants in front of the palace and a shriveled field of wild flowers. Ella knelt beside it and wove her fingers through the brittle stems. Tears leaked from her eyes. Where they fell, sprouted green leaves — small, but wick. She sang softly, sending healing vibrations along the ground. The dried mud creaked as dew formed on the dead plants and new sprouts forced their way timidly to the surface. Ella immediately felt exhausted.

"General Agnarsson." Two Hunters approached Oliver.

"Status, lads," Oliver said.

"Shadow is clear. It's moved off to sea," one Hunter said.

"Census shows five missing," the other Hunter said.

"Miss Ella." Ella recognized the Keeper's voice as he approached the group, clicking his walking stick along the footpath. His face waned to gray, and his wrinkles had deepened with weariness.

Ella stood to meet him.

"Miss Ella," he said again. "Megs has been taken."

Chapter 7

Devastation

Monday, September 4, 1899

Oliver dismissed the two Hunters, left Ella in the care of the Keeper and traveled alone to the center of town, where he first spotted the Shadow. He stood in Main Way, right outside Marilla's and surveyed the devastation. If it weren't for his training, he'd likely falter from the pain emanating from Alveland. This wasn't the time for faltering. Overnight, while he and Ella had been in Mannland, a two-mile path had been ripped through the town like a natural disaster. The path ran from north of the palace, through town, west of Marilla's and then veered off to sea.

According to his training, he knew that his next move was to walk the perimeter of devastation and examine it for clues. In the dim dawn, Oliver could see most of the stout-hearted, Palace Province elves already outside, healing their land. Wees and grown elves, alike, wept and wailed over their lost botanical loved ones.

"General."

Oh no. Oliver looked to the clouds for help.

"Did you find anything?" Oliver turned around and put eyes on his father, Commander Wagne Gleminol Agnarsson, Spirit of the Trees.

"Just got back."

"From where?" Oliver and his father matched in height and broad musculature, but that was where the similarities ended.

"Mannland. Saved a royal from the Shadow. She was outside the palace."

His father nodded, bobbing his dignified and neatly trimmed elvish beard. It was yet to harbor any signs of gray or thinning.

As he was forced to converse with his father, Oliver began to feel the exhaustion from his night of sleeplessness. Now he had a problem. His ever-present need — the thing that drove him out of bed every morning — was to keep Alveland safe and in its meant-state of peace and beauty. And his Alveland had just been attacked by its greatest enemy. He must get information about the Shadow. And if anyone would have information about the Shadow, it would be his father, the only elf among the Hunters who outranked him. But Oliver avoided interactions with his father. A conundrum, indeed.

His father quirked a side smile. Oliver knew he was waiting for him to swallow his pride and ask.

Oliver clenched his jaw. "Did you find anything?"

"The usual."

"Attracted to power, energy. Attack less than two hours. Less than ten taken?"

Commander Agnarsson nodded.

"Reports from inside?"

"Nothing new. Elvish vision impaired. Magic impaired. Labored breathing. Chilled. Depressed."

"Still think it's Klayden?"

"Or Burvanyek. Or Ohghee. Or all three"

"Any way to tell?"

"Does it matter?"

Oliver shrugged. "If it's all three, then nothing would be more powerful."

"Than three old elves who hate everything?" the Commander said.

"I've never heard of anyone," Oliver said.

"Some may say that a wee one who loves its tzi is more powerful."

"You said they hate everything. Do they hate themselves or everything else?"

"Where there is hate, it begins within one's own heart, directed at self," the Commander said.

"I'm going to walk the perimeter," Oliver said.

"I'll come, too."

Of all the rotten news. First the Shadow and now time alone with his father. Given the choice between the two, it may be a toss-up. Dealing with both on the same day just wasn't fair.

Oliver and his father began by the ocean, which was where the Shadow had entered the Palace Province. It was a warm day, so they let their brown Hunter cloaks open to the breeze. They didn't find very many clues from dead, floating fish, so they continued onward. They followed the devastation until they came to the Fainde River Bridge where they had to deviate from the path in order to cross the river. The Shadow path turned left toward the palace.

Oliver looked toward the east. There was the grassy knoll that cradled his favorite childhood play spot. He could feel his muscles flex with anticipation as he imagined himself running up the hill. He must have done that run more than a thousand times. He crouched low and studied the worn path beneath his feet. Just over the Shadow's border, the earth was brittle and lifeless. He reached his hand over it. It still had a chill. Saddened, he poured some of his own energy into the land and brought forth sprouts.

"Careful. Let the others do that. If you heal every attack you see, there will be nothing left of you."

Oliver knew that. He certainly didn't need his father to remind him. Still, this particular footpath seemed to be more a part of his heart than the earth. He wished he could heal the whole thing, but he didn't want to endure a lecture from his father.

"What objectives do you have for the Hunters?" Commander Agnarsson asked.

Oliver snapped to attention and accessed the organized part of his brain. "Main Objective: find the origin of the Shadow and destroy it. Sub Objectives: find the identity of the elf or elves controlling the Shadow. Find their motivation. Immediate Objectives: defend the defenseless against attack. Protect the palace. Protect the royals. Heal harm."

Commander Agnarsson nodded. "Action plan?"

"Hunters' Summit as soon as possible. Mappers to start charting the course of the Shadow and its next proposed location. Healer census and assistance. Land Restoration census and assistance."

"Tell the others."

Oliver sent a sound message to Haven, the Palace Province general, so she could tell her company. Then, he sent a sound message to the three Far Lands captains, of whom he was in charge. They would tell their quads. Oliver cracked his knuckles, eager to begin the hunt for bad guys. As long as he and his father weren't on the same task force, he'd be fine.

Chapter 8

Dietze

Sunday, September 3, 1899

The early morning moon glistened on the river and made little waves dance, inviting Ella in. She undressed, leaving her petticoats, dress, cloak and shoes in a pile and slid quietly into the water. Being early on in the fall, the water was much warmer than the air. She positioned herself just beneath a small rapid where the water pooled deeply. She floated on her back, letting her hair float freely down river. If only she could stay here forever.

Every memory she'd ever had with her river had been happy — except the one. She sat up and looked for her clothes. They were still there on the bank. She used her cloak as well as some magic to dry herself and redressed. She squeezed the excess water from her hair and twisted it into a large bun on the top of her head. It was such a simple joy, feeling the cool breeze on her neck.

Ella needed simple joys right now. When she had arrived in Alveland early this morning, she had rushed home. She felt relieved to find her parents at home and well. In fact, her mother and father were already outside, beginning the process of healing their land. ShaSha was hiding under her bed, still shivering from the attack. Ella tied on his chameleon's sweater she had crocheted for him. She also made a fold in her down bed blankets in case he wanted to burrow inside for more warmth.

She needed sleep after spending an all-nighter with Oliver in Mannland. But she had chosen to come to her river for comfort, first. She wanted to check it for devastation and hopefully feel its comfort.

Now that her swim was ended, Ella walked on soundless footsteps up the grassy knoll by where the rope swing hovered. She listened to the steady ripples and tried to figure out what to do. She sat on the riverbank and leaned against the friendly crepe myrtle tree, holding her fern flower necklace from Megs.

How could Megs have been taken? Despite her outward silence, her insides were screaming. How could this be real? If only she could go back in time to the moment they felt the first chill from the Shadow. She would have pulled Megs along home with her. Megs could have come to Mannland, too, and been safe. She released her blue-gray mix of sadness and anger into the tree and it whisked it away into the earth.

The tree's healing helped, but she still couldn't figure out what to do about Megs. She wasn't a Hunter. She wasn't brave. She was just a lady-elf who missed her best friend. Maybe a visit to the Keeper would be helpful. He loved both her and Megs like daughters. At least he'd understand.

First, Ella walked to Megs' dwelling in town. It was right in the path of the Shadow, and she shivered as she stood on her doorstep, ringing the bell. She let herself in. Dirty dishes lay on the table in the kitchen, as though she had just stepped out of the room. Ella heard a rustling in Megs' pantry. The hairs on Ella's neck stood on end. Her chest got tight and she gripped the countertop for stability. Surely it wasn't something evil. Surely it had nothing to do with Megs' disappearance. She took a steadying breath and followed the sound to the pantry. Three, two, one… throwing open the door she saw Dietze. Megs' yellow streaked tenrec scratching at some food bags that were on the floor.

"Poor little thing," Ella said. She knew Dietze must be hungry — Megs wouldn't have fed him since yesterday, before the Shadow attack. She set the tenrec in the hood of her cloak for the trip to the Keeper's dwelling.

Nestled in the foothills of the North Mountains, outside town the Keeper's property had hardly been affected by the attack — just a few wilted flowers. The Keeper was outside pruning the dead blossoms and healing his plants. Several new buds were already forming on his rose bushes.

"I was wondering if I'd be seeing you today, Miss Ella." The Keeper spoke to her without turning from his work. Ella could only see the back of his ornately embroidered, purple Keeper's cloak.

Ella sat quietly next to the garden. Two daisies blossomed near her. She tickled them gently with her fingers, grateful. Alveland needed to be saving its energy, though, for the healing from the devastation. Ella put Dietze in the garden so he could forage for worms and bugs.

"At your service, Miss Ella. How may I help?" the Keeper asked.

"What do we do about Megs?"

"Hm."

Ella waited patiently for an answer. She watched as he continued to clip and snip his flowers.

"The Hunters are trained to retrieve," the Keeper said.

Ella knew that. She didn't need to hear obvious facts. She didn't need him to tell her to wait. She needed him to tell her what to do with herself now that her friend was gone.

"I can tell by your energy, Miss Ella, that you are upset. And you are not content with my answer."

"I'm not up—" Arguing wouldn't do any good.

"Perhaps you can tell me why you feel riled up."

"Why?" Ella's foot tapped with impatience.

The Keeper shrugged as he moved to the next rose bush.

"You want me to stay here and wait for somebody to bring back my best friend?" Ella asked.

"Might be good not to trouble yourself."

"Not to trouble myself?" Ella couldn't believe what she was hearing. "I've already decided that I'm leaving. I've got to do something."

"Ah," the Keeper said.

Had she already decided that? When had she decided that?

"Where will you go?"

Ella didn't know.

"Or perhaps a better question is why haven't you left yet?"

"I'm not ready," Ella said. "I've got to prepare."

"Ah," the Keeper said again. "How will you prepare?"

"I'm not qualified to do anything. Except take Elvish Tea. I've got to figure out how to travel and fight. Oh gosh, am I going to need to fight? I've got to figure out where I should look for Megs. I don't even know where to start."

The Keeper turned and looked at her for the first time. He wore a small smile. Ella needed to ask the Keeper to stop messing around and give her some sound advice. She opened her mouth to sass him, when she realized that the Keeper had gotten her riled up on purpose.

She had given the sound advice to herself.

Chapter 9

Hunters' Summit

Monday, September 4, 1899

Oliver sat in the palace meeting hall. He stretched one leg long under the knotty, wooden banquet table and allowed the other leg to bounce. He watched all forty-four Hunters from the Palace Province and the Far Lands trickle in, along with the top Palace Advisors, King Frederick and Queen Sophia. Like the other Hunters, Oliver wore his short, brown, hooded linens. The Palace Advisors wore their long black silks. The King and Queen stood out in their royal velvets. Now that it had been about sixteen hours since the attack, the palace had returned to its normal temperature. Only the emotional chill still clung.

In between the attack and this evening's summit, Oliver had returned to his temporary quarters and slept. He was used to keeping an odd sleep schedule, or going days without sleep. It was part of the job. The sleep deprivation would have been worth it if they had gotten any closer to destroying the Shadow, but they hadn't.

His father stood up from his chair at the head of the banquet table. The room grew quiet enough to hear the sconces flickering against the stone walls. Commander Agnarsson began the meeting. First, he asked for a recapitulation of the events since the Hunters had arrived in the Palace Province. The team passed the task back and forth beginning with settling into their quarters, and ending with the clean-up efforts that had taken place that day.

Next, the Commander assigned Hunters to the home team and the retrieval team.

"Now for the next step," Commander Agnarsson said.

"Isn't it the same as always?" Celvin Pinwin Dopplesson, Spirit of Reptiles, one of the Hunter captains, spoke in his nasally voice.

"Could be," the Commander said. Oliver didn't know why he put up with such disrespectful interruptions from Celvin. He sure as hell wouldn't accept them.

"We have been following a problem around, though," Commander Agnarsson said. "It's time we come across a solution."

Celvin said something that Oliver didn't hear. Why he thought this was a personal conversation between himself and the Commander, Oliver didn't know. Oliver's leg jimmied faster. By the Spirits he hated the sound of Celvin's voice. He and Celvin had been Hunters together in the Far Lands since training school. Oliver knew that Celvin had hopes of becoming a general, like himself, some day. Celvin was probably just waiting for Oliver to get eaten by a Fang Dragon on one of their missions. Then he could take Oliver's place. Not that Celvin was malicious… he just tried too hard.

Oliver tried to focus on what his father was saying, but his emotions were running high. Oliver allowed a small amount of his black energy of annoyance to flow out of him. The Shadow had been terrorizing Alveland for two centuries. No one knew how to take down the Shadow and it really got under Oliver's skin. Without that information, all they could do was follow in its wake and clean up after it. He needed to get on the attack team, like usual, and head out after the Shadow. It was the only way he was going to collect more clues, and one day find out who was behind the Shadow.

"What do the Hunters usually do after an attack?" Advisor Argon Marina asked. His brown hair was so different from Ella's. Still, the curve of his profile made Oliver think of her.

"Get ready for the next one," answered Celvin.

The Commander finally silenced Celvin with a withering glare and respectfully addressed the Advisor's question. "The Hunters are usually divided into three teams. The home team stays behind to aid regrowth. The retrieval team searches for the Missing. The attack team goes ahead to the next location that is suspected for attack or follows the Shadow."

Oliver cracked his knuckles. He was always on the attack team because he was a fighter. In fact, he always led the attack team. After fielding many questions from the leaders, the Commander turned the meeting toward the actual dividing up of teams. He unrolled a parchment on which they were listed out for both the Palace Province RT and the Far Lands RT.

Oliver didn't hear his name, he rarely went out on retrievals. He didn't have particularly prominent tracking skills. No more than a regular, untrained elf anyway. He'd been on a few retrieval missions in the rougher terrain places. Not that anyone was ever actually found.

Next, Commander Agnarsson read the names of the home teams for both lands. Often, these were the older elves, or the elves who were injured and needed rest. Oliver knew that some of the Far Lands home team members were those with dear friends and family in Palace Province. Restoring Alveland was always a joy. These Hunters knew they were basically receiving a vacation. Plus, they'd be in the Palace Province, so they'd eat well, party often and feel appreciated.

"Now for the attack team." Commander Agnarsson pulled out his chair and sat down for the first time since the meeting began. He let out a sigh and looked around the room. "You'll be meeting on your own. Present me with maps tomorrow morning, and a list of supplies you'll need for travel and weather. Hopefully, you will leave within two days." Oliver was looking forward to it. His leg stopped bouncing and he began to relax into his chair.

"Excuse me." The interruption came from an elf seated in a small group near the King. They weren't Hunters or Advisors or members of the royal family. Oliver knew who they must be — the families of the five

Missing. The King had invited them as a way to care for them during this tragic time. "When will the Hunters search for the Missing?"

The elf's countenance was downcast, as were the others at the meeting representing their Missing loved ones. Two were the husbands of two Missing lady-elves. One lady-elf was there with her wee, representing her Missing husband who was an Advisor. Two were the parents of a young lass-elf, probably around fifteen. No one was there for Megs — her parents had died long ago.

The Commander crossed his fist across his chest and bowed to the families of the Missing in order to show them honor and respect. The families returned the gesture.

"The retrieval team will leave as soon as they have a safe trail out."

"Why can't they leave right away?" Marci, the mother of the lass-elf asked.

"The Shadow created a circle, and left the same way it entered. Its pathway out of Alveland was the same one it entered on. We must wait until the way has been repaired and searched for information," said the Commander.

"When was the last time you found a group of the Missing?" Marci asked.

The Commander cleared his throat and looked down at the table. "Never," he said.

"Is there anything we can do?" Marci asked.

"Please come to my quarters, day or night, if you sense the Spirit of your loved one who is Missing.

Otherwise, there is no action for you to take," the Commander said.

Suddenly, the door to the meeting hall banged open and clanged against the wall. Ella burst inside. This could not be good.

―――

Oliver saw that Ella's hands were shaking, and she hesitated before stepping into the room. Commander Agnarsson stood, as did King Frederick. Ella had changed since their escape into the human realm. She looked rested and refreshed, wearing a casual, midnight-blue dress made from the traditional elvish silk, over several petticoats. Her curls were loosely tied behind her neck.

"Lady Ella," King Frederick said. "Is everything all right?"

Ella took a cautious step forward and curtsied. "Your Majesty."

The King inclined his head.

All the Hunters, all the Advisors, the King and Queen all stared at Ella. She opened her mouth as though to speak, but nothing came out. Finally she clenched her hands by her sides.

"Megs is missing. I know you'll go after her, soon. May I come with you?" She closed her eyes while she spoke. Her cheeks flushed.

Oliver looked at his father. He didn't look surprised by Ella's outburst. His father never looked surprised by anything, though. "No disrespect, Lady Ella, but why would we take you?"

"I am the only family Megs has," she said. "I cannot accept 'no' as your answer." Ella looked over at the families of the Missing, seated by the King, and she knew it to be true. There was another reason Ella needed to be accepted into the Hunter's team, but she couldn't quite explain it to herself, let alone to Commander Agnarsson.

The Commander looked at the King. Ella lifted her chin. It was easy for Oliver to believe that she was once destined to be the Princess of Alveland. It was a shame she wouldn't be. Emil must be smitten with this human to refuse Ella. Of course, it was hard for Oliver to wrap his head around that idea because he'd never been that smitten with anyone — not really.

"Please," Ella's commanding voice was laced with desperation. "Can I just go with you? Is there not a group of you that will go and look for the Missing?"

"You'd be a liability," Commander Agnarsson said. "You can't defend yourself. Our Hunters would be responsible for your safety as well as the search for the Missing."

"I know how to fight." Ella took another step toward the group and motioned toward Oliver. "I learned to spar with your son. I'd just need to refresh."

Commander Agnarsson looked at Oliver, but his expression was unreadable. Then he looked at the King, who raised his royal eyebrows. Finally, he looked back at

Ella, who seemed to have gained momentum and would not let it rest.

"I won't be a liability, I'm sure of it. Your Hunters can leave me in harm's way if need be. My life will be in my own hands. Commander, I cannot stay behind."

Commander Agnarsson exhaled and put his hands in the pockets of his cloak. "It's out of the question, Lady Ella."

"It's not Lady Ella, any more. It's Miss Ella. Sir." Ella's eyes had narrowed.

Oliver noticed that King Frederick's cheeks flushed.

"This meeting is adjourned," said Commander Agnarsson.

Chapter 10

The Silent Treatment

Tuesday, September 5, 1899

In the first light of morning, Ella was perched on the garden wall, eating one of Mitsy's breakfast rolls and waiting for the Prince. She pulled the roll apart in little flakey bits and ate them, not taking her eyes off the castle doors.

Ella had been dumped by the Prince. Then her home was attacked by the Shadow. Then Oliver whisked her away to Mannland during which time her best friend was kidnapped. She went an entire day and night without sleep. After her chat with the Keeper, she had to wait all day long for the evening Hunters' Summit, so she marched herself home and took a much-needed nap. When she awoke, rested, she had Mitsy help her dress for the Summit. As Mitsy did her hair and make-up, Ella thought of at least ten reasons why she was unqualified to search for Megs.

You have no useful tracking skills, the Hunters won't want you, and it's going to be dangerous… Brittany had reminded her. With those points acknowledged, Ella went to the castle, making sure not to tell Mitsy where she was going. There was no way Mitsy would let her interrupt a Hunters' Summit. Her parents had trained Mitsy better than that.

Ella got so nervous about going to the Hunters' Summit she threw up in the garden in front of the Grand Step. She wasn't even sure the palace guard would still let her inside the castle. Nevertheless, it seemed that after being engaged to Emil for over a hundred years, she was still allowed admittance. (Probably in case she and Emil wished to work out their relationship.) The guards escorted her to the back of the castle on the main floor in order to locate the Hunters. They patiently watched her as she paced the hallway trying to convince herself to enter the meeting. What could she possibly say to the Hunters to convince them to take her along? All Ella had ever done was prepare for being a royal lady. She wouldn't even take herself if she was in their position.

The only way she convinced herself to enter was to do it at a bit of a run, so she ended up banging the door to the conference hall almost off its hinges. And just in case she wasn't feeling uncomfortable enough, her ex-father-in-law-to-be (the King) was in the meeting as well. His face, Oliver's face and the faces of her bewildered parents were the only faces that would come into focus. The sea of brown Hunters and the sea of black Advisors were intimidating, wobbling around in her vision like an ocean and making her nauseous again.

Ella hardly remembered the words when she argued her point with the Commander of the Hunters, but she did remember when he said he would not allow her to go on the mission, dismissed the meeting and left.

Now, it was Monday morning and Ella waited, sure that Emil would come through that door, soon.

"Good morning." Ella had spotted Emil and lurched toward him.

"What are you doing here?"

"I need your help."

"Oh?" Emil continued on his walking course down the Grand Step and along the palace footpath.

"I need you to get me on the retrieval team with the Hunters."

"You're not a Hunter."

"I know."

"I have no control over Hunter teams."

"You're the prince of all of Alveland. Throw a princely temper tantrum for me."

Emil gave her a deadpan look.

"You owe me."

"I owe you?"

"Yes."

"How long am I going to owe you?"

Ella shrugged and took another bite of her roll. "Probably forever."

Emil rolled his eyes.

"Well," Ella's cheeks flushed, "you broke off my engagement. To a prince."

Emil stopped walking. "Ella."

He said her name so serenely, like a father soothing a wee.

"I will marry you, if you want me to."

"Shut up," Ella said. "That makes it worse. Then I can't even be mad at you."

Emil chuckled. "Practically speaking, how do you suggest I help you?"

Ella shrugged. "Talk to the Commander for me. Or your dad. Or Oliver. Talk to someone."

Emil sighed and rubbed his temples. "I can't promise you anything,"

"Thank you!" He hadn't said no. Ella patted him on the head and left before he could.

She moved on to her next mission without enthusiasm. Not that she had wanted to confront her ex-boyfriend, but at least Emil was reasonable.

Now, however, she had to see Oliver. She procrastinated by singing to her orchards and took an apple to eat while she crossed the Fainde River Bridge. Ella noticed a storm cloud forming just off the coast.

When Ella arrived at Oliver's, she had no idea whether or not she should knock. She sat on the steps of his dwelling and twirled her fern flower necklace, trying to decide. Ella's head snapped up when footsteps approached. Oliver wasn't even at home, he had been out and was walking down the road towards her. He scowled when he saw her.

"I need your help," said Ella.

"No," said Oliver.

"Yes," said Ella.

Oliver walked past her and into his dwelling.

Even though she wasn't invited in, Ella followed. His dwelling smelled like the forest of the Palace Province—probably because of all the wood. This temporary dwelling was simple, yet beautiful. It had lots of pale wood at right angles, but the braided rug in the sitting room made it inviting.

"I need you to convince your father to let me come look for Megs."

"No," Oliver said again.

Oliver had to help her. He and Emil were her last hope.

Oliver was not being a gracious host. He pulled out a handful of nuts from his pantry and violently chomped on them with his back to Ella. Such rudeness made Ella's cheeks flush. Not only had he not invited her in, but he hadn't offered her refreshment. His father would have been horrified at his behavior.

When Oliver's tzi entered the kitchen, Ella jumped in fear. She had forgotten that his tzi was a bobcat named Onyx. Why he named it Onyx, she didn't know. Maybe to match his perpetual black mood. He prowled around the room on deadly silent feet and narrowed his eyes at her. He twitched his fuzz-tipped ears in displeasure, then rubbed against Oliver's legs. Oliver fed him meat from the cold box.

Ella scowled back at Oliver. Maybe the sheer annoyance of her presence would work in her favor. Oliver took out another handful of nuts and ate them in front of Ella's nose. Ella took a breath to say something, but couldn't figure out what to say. She couldn't yell at him — she needed his help.

Oliver threw his cloak over his shoulder and left his house, again.

"What is wrong with you?" Ella ran after him.

Oliver didn't answer, but just kept walking. Ella followed. She wasn't used to people walking away from her and treating her rudely. She was used to getting her way — she had almost been the Princess, after all. Oliver walked right out of town and over the Fainde River Bridge. He was using silent warfare on her. He probably thought Ella would get sick of following him around. He was in for a surprise.

Oliver walked in front of the palace to the ivy wall as he had on the night they had escaped from the Shadow.

"What are you doing?" Ella didn't want to go back into the human realm. The energy was oppressive. It was cold, and not in a good way.

Oliver, continuing to ignore Ella, yanked open the door and entered the tunnel. Fine. Ella would follow him wherever he went, even into Mannland. And she would do it silently, just like Oliver. She would beat him at his own warfare. They took the familiar tunnel to the portal and passed through it. Then they crossed the open field and came to town, just like last time. And then they entered town and walked until they, once again, came to John Gregor's Old Pub.

It was ghostly quiet. It felt nothing like last night with the band playing and the crowded dance floor.

Ella followed Oliver to one of the many empty tables in the back of the building. He kept his cloak on and his hood up. When a waitress came over, Oliver ordered a beer and a paper. Ella did the same. They sipped and read silently for hours. The two elves in disguise stubbornly sat at that table until lunch, at which point Ella's stomach began to grumble. Oliver ordered a fish salad roll and another ale. Ella did the same. They continued to sit and read throughout the afternoon, only interacting with their waitress, and refusing to make eye contact with each other.

Humans began filtering in as evening approached. Ella wondered if Oliver had to be back in the elvish realm for any more meetings with the Hunters before they left. Obviously not. The front doors swung open once more and a burst of cold air and laughter entered the building. A group of jolly friends entered, maybe already inebriated. The one in the middle looked familiar. Ella gasped, the first sound she'd made in a while. She recognized him as Dagur, the man she had met on the night of the Shadow attack.

Ella got an idea. She grinned at Oliver and shrugged out of her elvish cloak. Then, she adjusted the bodice of her dress and let her curls fall forward over her shoulders. Oliver continued to scowl at his paper. Ella slid out of the booth and made quite the fuss of fixing the skirts of her dress and petticoats. Then she glanced over her shoulder at Dagur's group of friends while she hung her cloak on the hook by their table. She caught the attention of one of Dagur's friends and waved. Then she sat down again. That should do it.

Before long, she heard footsteps approaching. She hoped Oliver was paying attention.

"Miss Ella?"

Ella looked up into Dagur's dimpled smile. Her heart fluttered.

"Won't you and your brother join us at our table?"

"We couldn't possibly," Oliver said.

"I must insist. It's my birthday," Dagur said.

Ella took Dagur's arm and followed him over to a large, round table. His friends shuffled so she could sit right next to Dagur. Even in Mannland, Ella could feel Oliver's seething black energy. He followed her to Dagur's table and sat right next to Ella, as she assumed he would. Once seated, Ella turned her back on Oliver and gave her undivided attention to Dagur.

Chapter 11

Oliver's Very Bad Day

Tuesday, September 5, 1899

Oliver had led them to the human realm hoping to take advantage of the lack of energy and Ella's lack of comfort to drive her away from this ridiculous task of traveling with the Hunters. He was trained in surviving without Alveland's vivaciousness. Ella wasn't. So how was she winning?

By the Spirits, he was a trained Hunter. He knew that twelve of the humans in this bar were armed. He knew that there were three exits in the building and which one was closest. He knew eight easy ways to kill the human Ella was talking to and yet, he could not get Ella to stop talking to him. Talking? Flirting.

He watched as her hand shot out and rested on the human's arm. He could feel the energy of attraction rolling off of him as he looked at Ella as though she were something to eat.

"Let me get my overcloak." Oliver heard Ella say that.

Ella took a drink of her alcohol, purchased for her by the human. Then she turned toward Oliver and rifled through her bag.

"What do you think you're doing?" Oliver whispered.

"I'm getting ready to go," whispered Ella.

"With Dagur?"

Ella shrugged.

"Don't you know what he'll expect of you?"

Ella glared at Oliver.

Oliver felt his temper rise. Angry-gray energy bubbled at his core. "I'm not getting you in with the Hunters."

"Have a good night." Ella patted Oliver on the cheek, rather hard.

Oliver clenched his teeth at the irritating gesture. He watched as Ella tied on her overcloak and turned back to Dagur. Would she really go with him? Oliver grabbed Ella's arm.

She looked at him expectantly.

"I'll talk to my pa." The words tasted like defeat.

"About me." Ella sat down to negotiate.

"About you."

"And you'll explain why I'm essential to this mission."

"Fine." Oliver released Ella's arm.

Ella spun around and gave Dagur a quick kiss on the cheek. "Ollie's just reminded me that I'm supposed to help out our father early tomorrow. So sorry, but I have to go."

Dagur pressed her hand. Oliver's eyes locked on the physical contact. The human was disappointed. Dagur urged Ella to reconsider, but she didn't concede. She stood and dressed in her overcloak. Oliver and Ella finally left John Gregor's. This was his own fault.

Oliver pulled his elvish cloak tighter around him, but the chill got in anyway. It was way too cold in the human realm. Oliver stormed off in the direction of the portal. Ella could keep up or not, he didn't care.

Without warning, Ella ran in front of Oliver. She spun toward him, placed one hand on his arm and one hand behind his neck. Then, she swept his feet out from under him with her slippered foot. His taken-down body left an indentation in the early snow.

"What in the name of the Spirits are you doing?" A muscle ticked in Oliver's jaw.

Ella looked amused. If she was intimidated by him, she didn't show it.

By the time Oliver got to his feet, Ella was ready with a two-handed takedown.

Oliver grunted as his face hit the ground.

"Blech." Oliver got up again, this time spitting out snow. "You have no reasonable bones in your body," said Oliver. "I saved you from the Shadow. I saved you from a night with a man. In a different realm."

This time, when Oliver stood up, she did a choke hold takedown.

Oliver untied his elvish cloak. Ella tossed hers aside as well.

If Ella wanted to settle the score with Glima, then he'd settle it. Past experience taught him that Ella didn't fight with her body. He checked his hip against hers and wrapped his leg around hers. It was as if she saw it coming. Ella tucked into Oliver's side and escaped. By the time he turned to face her, she was already in position to do another two-handed takedown.

Oliver finally saw a moment's opening and took it to conquer Ella. He squatted beside her and did an over the shoulder throw down, gently, of course. When she returned to her feet, both elves stood and gathered themselves.

"Maybe I was a bit unreasonable," Ella said.

"You think?" It was about time she said something uncrazy.

Ella crouched and swiped her leg behind his feet. Oliver ended up on his ass in the snow once again.

Oliver sighed. "Maybe I was a bit unreasonable, too."

———

Once inside Alveland, with reluctance in every step, Oliver led Ella into the palace courtyard, off of which sat his father's suite — it was where he always stayed when the Hunters traveled to the Palace Province. Emil was already in his study, speaking on Ella's behalf. With two reputable elves speaking for her, the Commander agreed to take Ella along on the hunt.

Oliver comforted himself by remembering that at least she'd be on the retrieval team and not with him.

"Oliver, you trade with Kyle," Commander Agnarsson said.

"Sir?" asked Oliver. "Kyle is a retriever."

"You travel on the retrieval team with Miss Ella to help her practice her self-defense."

"Sir?"

Commander Agnarsson clapped Oliver on the shoulder and headed back to his quarters.

This could not be happening. Oliver was a fighter, not a retriever. Training and rank forbade Oliver from arguing with his father. At least not in front of other elves. He bit his bottom lip to keep from an outburst.

"One last thing," Commander Agnarsson turned in his doorway. "I'll travel with the retrieval group as well."

Chapter 12

Moving Out

Wednesday, September 6, 1899

It was officially time to panic. Ella had gotten what she wanted. She had gotten Oliver and Emil to convince Commander Agnarsson to include her in the Hunters' search. But she wasn't going to be allowed to hop on their ship and dally along for the ride. Oh no, she offered to become a fighting member of the Hunters so they didn't have to feel responsible for her. What was she thinking? What qualified her to join the Hunters? Nothing. Not one thing. Not the tea, not the gowns, not the bowing or the jewelry, not the tarts or the dance lessons. Nothing. Should be a disaster, Brittany added. Oh, and Megs was still missing.

Mitsy entered her room and placed her fragile cup and saucer on her cherry wood bedside table. The hot, herbal tea steamed soothingly and Ella took a sip.

"Will ya be takin' breakfast in the dining hall or in yer room this mornin' Miss Ella?" Mitsy shuffled over to the lacy curtains and pushed the pink fabric behind their hooks.

Ella just stared at Mitsy.

"Everything all right, Miss Ella?"

"I'm taking breakfast at University."

"Speak again?"

"I'm taking breakfast at University," Ella said. "And all my meals. That's where the Hunters are meeting. That's where they're training, so, I will too."

"But Miss Ella, you've never been on your own, before." Mitsy pointed out a true thing.

"Yes, well, I'm going to be on my own, now." Ella opened the trunk at the foot of her bed and began putting clothes in it. "I'm ninety-four years old. It's about time."

"Do your parents know?" Mitsy asked.

"No," Ella said.

Mitsy inched toward the door. "Let me know if you need anything."

Mitsy was going to tattle on her. That was fine. Let her tell them. Let them find out. She, Ella Manweli Marina, Spirit of Flowers was leaving home and striking out on her own. Most elves strike out on their own around the time they come of age. In Mannland that is usually around age eighteen, but in Alveland it was age one hundred because elves age so much slower than humans.

"I'm doing this for Megs," she told ShaSha, who was very slowly creeping across the embroidered bedspread.

ShaSha paused and looked at Ella with one of his eyes.

"Of course you can come," Ella said. "But not if we do anything dangerous."

Satisfied with her answer, the chameleon continued his creep across the bedcovers.

"You can't go, wee Ella. You've just broken up with Emil. I still think we can work out the marriage thing for you if you'll only let us." Maria Marina wrung her slender hands.

Mitsy had outed her. Both of her parents were in her room, blocking the door and trying to talk her out of leaving. If they weren't so loving, it would be easy to go against their wishes. But they were. Ella had always found her greatest comfort in the smile of her father. But it was time for her to go. Maybe even past time.

"First, I'm not wee. Second, I don't want to marry Emil. Third… I'm leaving. Think of your life, Ma. You are a respected member of the Advisors, yes? Your currency is overflowing. Mine has all but stopped. And my best friend is among the Missing."

"Be reasonable, Ellie-Boo," Argon pleaded. "If you insist on going to look for Megs, do it from here. Send her a sound message."

Ella gave her father a deadpan look. As though she hadn't tried that. Every day since the disappearance. She wanted her parents to see her as someone other than 'Ellie-Boo'. But to be sure, she'd never been anyone other than 'Ellie-Boo'. It was definitely time to go.

"Let us come up with a more rational idea, shall we?" Maria asked. "Leave the search to the Hunters. Surely they'll take care of it."

"No one's ever been found, Ma," Ella said. Besides, she was in too deep, now that she'd convinced the Commander to train her. She'd have to go, wouldn't she?

Ella knew her parents meant well from their protests, they only wanted her welfare. But they had always conveyed to her that the only way they thought she could achieve welfare was with their help. It was time to see if that was true. Ella needed to try to accomplish something on her own. Maybe she should have picked something simpler than rescuing someone from the Shadow.

Despite their pleas to stay, Ella finally did it. She latched her trunk, pushed it past her parents and bumped it down the staircase. She heaved and hauled open the front door and shoved the trunk outside.

"At least take some currency." Ella's father handed her a small sack of coins.

She stared at the bag while an argument raged within her. She was tired of depending on others. She had always depended on her parents for everything, except for her future. For her future she had depended on Emil. She needed to start depending on herself, and the capabilities with which Alveland had blessed her.

Practically speaking, she had not asked for the money, and she needed to pay for transportation for herself and her trunk to University. She held out her hand and allowed the sack to clink into her palm. She kissed her father and mother on their cheeks. Then, she pressed her middle three fingers to each of their foreheads, conveying her love and well wishes in her absence.

That was the hardest part. Now, all she had to do was walk out the door. She dragged her trunk downtown where she hired a driver to drive her and her trunk across the West Lands to University. Mitsy, her mother and her father all stood on their stone porch as she rode away. Ella looked at the towering Advisor dwelling in which she had grown up. It rivaled the palace in beauty. And lined up across the front porch balcony leaned her loved ones, looking worried.

Feeling very independent, Ella marched her trunk up to the building labeled Central Office. The desk clerk sat menacingly at the oversized, wooden desk, cloaked in black. Ella liked the look and feel of the building, but not the energy from the desk clerk. The building had wood from floor to ceiling, as was customary for elvish dwellings to be. The back wall of the building had even been built around some rather large tree trunks. Their branches hung below the ceiling, and Ella could see their leaves dangling above them.

"I'm here to meet and train with the Hunters." Ella spoke with false confidence. She hid her shaking hands behind her back.

"You can check into the Amarind Building. Room two-one-three." The desk clerk was an older elf — definitely over fourteen hundred years old. The lines on the tree trunk barks seemed to match those in her face. "How will you pay for your housing?"

"Pay?" Ella asked. The sack of money her father had loaned her was enough for the ride over and perhaps a few meals, but not enough to pay rent at University. That didn't matter, she wasn't going to rely on money from her parents any more. "Can I get back to you on that?"

The desk clerk looked at her with great annoyance over a pair of dark-rimmed, half-moon spectacles. She took out a paper, wrote in large letters, *two-one-three payment due*, and placed it in a file on her desk. Ella had to figure out payment — fast. She was fairly certain that this particular desk clerk would not forget about her, soon.

"I'll just get this approved with the general," the clerk said.

Oh no. The general was Oliver. Why did she need his approval?

"General, I have an elf, here, for training without housing payment." *Pop*.

"University is full." *Pop*. "I'll be right there." *Pop*, came Oliver's reply.

Wonderful. Ella drummed her fingers on the desk and stood awkwardly next to the desk clerk. The clerk's mouse tzi scuttled down her arm and onto the desk. It sniffed Ella's moving fingers before returning to the clerk's shoulder. Ella could tell by her energy that she was a river spirit, dark and powerful, with a freedom lurking somewhere behind her tied-back exterior. Ella wanted her to let down her hair from its bun or do something to make herself more approachable. The dark and powerful came through loud and clear, but Ella could have used a bit more freedom at this moment.

"Oh." Oliver's disappointment radiated through the single syllable. Onyx, his dark-spirited bobcat, slunk into the room behind him.

Ella glared at both of them.

"She's acceptable." Oliver tried to duck out of the room before he had even entered all the way.

"General, does she need a down payment?"

"She couldn't be expected to leave one."

Ella crossed her arms. "I can leave a down payment."

"Now?" Oliver asked.

"Not in this moment, but—"

Oliver exhaled loudly and addressed the clerk. "The Commander has accepted her. She needs housing, so let her in."

"I'm putting her in the Amarind Building."

"Fine." With one final frown, Oliver left. Onyx, frowned at her, too, then followed after Oliver.

Ella remembered only one time when Oliver had spoken to her without a scowl. It was when they were wee. Long before he left. Oh well, she wouldn't expect it to happen a second time. Ella took the key from the clerk and hauled her trunk outside to find the Amarind Building. She'd just add, 'Get A Currency Assignment' to her to-do list. Right before, 'Rescue Best Friend From the Shadow' and 'Learn How to Be a Hunter'. And let's be honest, 'Learn to Take Care of Herself'.

Ella unpacked the few belongings she had brought in one half of the room. There were two beds, so she guessed that she would have a room-mate at some point. Although, she didn't know who. Oliver said the Hunter University was full. She unloaded Dietze and ShaSha from her cloak and gave them each a spot on her bed. Next, she grabbed her silken side bag and walked back into town to see about a job.

She'd start with Marilla's. It was one of her favorite places to take her leisure, so it would be a bonus if she could get paid to be there. Ella strode in with confidence and slid onto a barstool.

"Miss Ella." Bear attended to her immediately, as usual, with his very large grin.

"Bear, I need a currency provider."

"Where ya lookin?" Bear asked.

"Here." Ella was surprised that that wasn't abundantly clear.

"Oh." Bear's face fell. "Well, what's yer experience?"

Ella started sweating beneath her dress. It was one of her nicer dresses that she always wore with three petticoats.

"Can ya wash dishes?" asked Bear.

"I've never washed a dish," said Ella.

"Served tables before?"

Ella shook her head.

"Maybe you can talk with Benton over here, down the bar. He's looking for someone in his shop."

Bear introduced Benton and Ella.

"Ella's looking for a job," said Bear.

"Need someone in my shop," said Benton.

"Perfect," said Ella. "What kind of shop?"

"Iron," said Benton.

"Oh," said Ella.

"Have ye done any ironwork before?"

"No."

"Stoked a fire?"

"No."

"Perhaps yer good with animals?"

"Yes!" Finally, something she could relate to. "My tzi is a chameleon."

"Mm. But ye know how to drive a donkey?"

"Well… no."

Benton scratched his bearded chin. "I'll certainly let you know if I need you, Miss Ella. In the meantime, I think I need to hire an ironworker."

Ella left Marilla's only slightly deflated. This was still her day. She still had a new home, hope of joining the Hunters, and most important, a step toward finding Megs. How hard could it be to find a job?

How hard, indeed.

At first, Main Way welcomed her in its usual way. The porches of each elvish business jutted out at different angles, depicting the character of each shop. But as she knocked on each door, she grew more discouraged. It felt like her old home was trying to push her out. The seamstress asked her if she knew how to sew, which was a reasonable question. She had to tell the truth, though. Why would she ever have learned how to sew when Mitsy mended everything? No one needed her skill set.

Or lack of skill set, said Brittany.

She wandered down the quiet road in which Megs' shop was located. She cupped her hands against the window, but it was so dark inside she couldn't see anything.

Megs wouldn't even hire you, said Brittany.

She absolutely would. She'd hire her because they were friends. Maybe.

Ella needed a break from all this rejection. Up until Emil had broken off their engagement, her currency was full. The role of Alveland Princess produced a great deal of currency. Now, she needed an assignment to provide her with currency. In Alveland, the more closely related to your elvish calling your assignment, the more your currency. Many young elves her age had unfulfilling assignments which provided little currency, because they had not found their true elvish calling. She wandered away from town and up the skinny, dirt path that led to the foothills. When she reached the bottom of the Keeper's land plot, she breathed in fresh air and let the sunlight warm her face.

"Miss Ella." The Keeper used her new, non-royal title, remembering her change in status. She thought of the time she saw Emil sitting at Marilla's with Karina and felt a pang in her chest.

"Still looking for Miss Megs?" The Keeper was tending his vegetable garden. It was harvest time, and he had two large baskets full of colorful leafies.

"Looking for a currency assignment, today, actually." Ella sat amongst the hedges and removed her slippers.

"Unusual."

"Yes, indeed. The Princess of Alveland never needed a currency assignment."

"Of course."

"Now I must pay for University Housing with the Hunters. The Hunters are going to train me and take me with them to look for Megs. And the other Missing."

"I see."

"And I have to pay rent."

"Your ma and pa are not paying?"

"I don't want them to. I've never done anything on my own."

"A false statement, I think."

"Besides have tea."

"You've done more than that."

Ella shrugged.

"Speaking of tea, Miss Ella, shall we have some?"

"Do you have Merkleberry?"

"Don't I always?"

Ella's lips involuntarily formed into a smile and she jumped up from her spot in the hedges and went inside the Keeper's dwelling.

"As it happens, Mrs Holden walked by my dwelling earlier today." The Keeper swirled the steam from his tea around his finger. He formed it, first into a rose, and then into a dragon.

"Oh?" Ella sipped her tea and played with her tasseled napkin.

"She's looking for a new nanny."

"Really?" Ella wasn't excited about nannying. But it probably didn't take any specific skills. Perhaps she had a chance.

"You ought to send her a sound message," said the Keeper.

Maybe she ought.

Chapter 13

Glima

Wednesday, September 6, 1899

Oliver needed to blow off some steam or he'd punch a hole through a wall. He had arrived at Marilla's promptly at eight, ordered a beer and carried it downstairs to the Glima pit. Oliver signed up with Neiman, the gatekeeper to the Palace Province Glima tournament. He looked like a gatekeeper. Facial hair plagued his face and a huge scar sliced across his right cheek. The funniest thing about Neiman, though, was that he was a Flower Spirit. Oliver had never seen him fight anyone, only manage sign-ups.

Oliver climbed in the ring across from his first opponent and immediately felt at home. A surge of adrenaline pulsed through his body. Simply put, he felt better. He ceremonially grabbed his opponent's forearms to begin the fight. They started their traditional footwork. Oliver spun around on his opponent and pulled his legs out from under him. Finally, he buried his opponent's face into the ground and backed away for the victory. The Shadow and Ella and his father all moved to the back of his mind. Thank Alveland for Glima.

Now, just three rounds from the end of the tournament, Oliver shoved Benji's face in the dirt and backed away for the victory. There, now that that was done, he could towel off the sweat, dripping from his chin and down his abs. Glima made everything better. Even the fact that his dad had removed him from attack. Even the fact that he had to work with his father. Even the fact that Ella had made a fool of him in the human realm — twice.

Speaking of Ella, Oliver glanced up from the Glima pit to the bar on the main level of Marilla's. He watched Bear slide a frothy ale down the bar to her. That pudgy fool had been in love with Ella from the moment he laid eyes on her. He wasn't the only one, either. Ella thanked him, then turned her attention to the Glima pit. Her eyes met Oliver's and the smile disappeared from her face. What did she have to be sour about? She got what she wanted, like always.

Oliver saw Ella slide into a chair at a high table overlooking the wooden rail into the Glima pit. Oliver followed her movements discreetly. Why should he care where Ella sat, anyway? He didn't.

When Ella looked down into the Glima pit a second time, Oliver jerked his focus back to Benji. He had three rounds to go after Benji to win the night's belt. He would, of course, bow out before the last round. The Province Belt Holder always bowed out during the weekday tournaments. Oliver sat on his stool in the corner of the pit.

A female elf lurked behind him, making eyes at Oliver. She was leggy with chestnut curls which created a sultry curtain around her body. Her dress was cut almost to her belly button. Oliver didn't mind. He'd need to get his focus off these Palace Province lass-elves, if he was going to beat Benji, let alone get to the night's championship round.

Fortunately, Ella didn't dress like that. If she did, Oliver wouldn't stand a chance of concentration. No, she preferred to wear puffy royal gowns with all those ridiculous petticoats. Tonight, for example, she had on a rose-colored puff gown. And the petticoats made her look like a gum ball. This was no time for women or gumballs. This was fight time.

Hand drums thrummed from the house band. Oliver set his drink on the high table and lay the Glima belt next to it. Marilla's had an open floor on each level. The basement was the Glima pit, and the other two were for dancing. Now that the night's Glima tournament was finished, he was bathed and ready for other forms of evening entertainment. The musicians played the folk music for a group dance. It wasn't difficult for Oliver to find the elf who had been watching him earlier. She had certainly dressed for the occasion and put in her time, watching all ten rounds of Glima. He led her by the hand onto the dance floor. Slow drum beats led them in plodding steps as they turned and ducked and switched partners around the circle.

He liked his mystery partner. Her name was Betsy. He also liked his next several partners — all blushing and smiley. He spun to find his next partner who would be his last of the dance.

"Oliver." The new partner was Ella. She looked as surprised to see him as he was to see her. For some reason he thought she'd be home drinking tea or something. But of course, it made sense that she would stay after the tournament for a distraction from Megs' disappearance. They all came to Marilla's for distraction.

"Ella." He always said her name with an air of scolding. He pulled her tiny waist as close as her skirts would allow. She felt breakable in his hands. Of course, this was the same Ella who had blackmailed him into bringing her on their rescue mission and then fought him in the snow in the human realm. She was not breakable.

Ella's curls brushed his hand when she ducked under his arm as the dance steps required. As they both spun away to return to their original partners, he caught the faint scent of honeysuckle. He wanted to turn back and smell it again. Of course, he couldn't.

Afterward, Oliver led Betsy back to his table. Even though he was drinking with Betsy, he turned towards the bar to see if Ella was there. Her back was to him and she was talking to several elves at the bar. He had gotten a bizarre feeling while they were dancing. It wasn't an entirely new feeling. He tried to think of other things instead of what he was thinking about. Ella had always, always been Emil's lass, even when they were little. Even now that they had broken up, she was still Emil's former betrothed. Ella was definitely the last elf in Alveland he would ever court.

Midnight came and went. As the bar began to clear, Oliver spotted his father down the bar, enjoying a draught with an advisor from the Palace Province. It was Advisor Marina, Ella's father. Oliver swallowed the last of his ale and sauntered over to him. He stood in his father's eyeline, crossed his arms and waited.

"Excuse me, would you, Advisor?"

Mr Marina grabbed his overcloak and went for a walk.

"General?" Commander Agnarsson addressed his son.

"Sir." Oliver sat down.

"From your energy… a problem." It wasn't a question.

"You put me on the wrong team."

"Mm."

"I have attack team skills, Pa. I'm not a tracker."

"We have an addition."

Oliver rolled his eyes. Of course this was all Ella's fault. Oliver tried to picture Ella in her elvish slippers and puffy gown on a Hunting mission. The thought was ridiculous.

Commander Agnarsson shrugged. "You are most familiar with her out of all of us."

"She's just an elf, Pa, not a menace."

Commander Agnarsson's mouth quirked into a small smile. "Remains to be seen."

"Pa, don't make me beg."

"I wouldn't dare."

"But I still have to retrieve."

"It's an assignment."

"Come on, Pa."

"You could always request a formal change."

Oliver rolled his eyes again. Whenever a Hunter requested a formal change, they were bunked. Sometimes for years until they could be reassigned to an entirely different quad. His father knew he would never do that. He could never sit out.

Commander Agnarsson took a long drink of his ale and then stood next to his stool. "See you at Summit."

Oliver watched him don his overcloak and turn to leave.

"Leaving always was your move," Oliver said.

The Commander's footsteps paused for a moment to acknowledge the comment, but he didn't stop his trajectory out the heavy, wooden front door of Marilla's.

Chapter 14

Hunter Training

Thursday, September 7, 1899

Ella knocked and wiped her sweaty palms on the front of her dress. It was gray silk and matched the Holding's graywood front door. The door was rounded, like many elvish doors. This rounded architecture represented the eternal path all elves are privileged to walk over their very long lives. Ella tried to calm her nerves by reminding herself that she had known Mr and Mrs Holding for years. She had interacted with them several times before as they were both Royal Council Members, like her parents.

Ella assumed the Holdings needed to hire someone who would function similarly to Mitsy. Could she be Mitsy? Mitsy worked hard. As a wee, she spent the day with Mitsy and saw her family for dinner. Once she came of age, Mitsy had become her lady's maid.

Why was no one coming to the door? As she waited, Ella glanced up at the early morning sun, shooting through the early morning chill. The air dust danced happily in the beams of lighting, searching for a place to land. Ella stood among the Advisor dwellings, just two blocks from where she had grown up. She allowed her gaze to travel east, toward the elevated buildings of University in the distance. She didn't live in the Advisor dwellings any more. The thought of being a University student filled her chest with pride and she breathed in a refreshing breath of salty, sea air.

Now if only she could find a job, so she could actually afford to live on her own.

There was a scuffle and some yelling and the door was finally opened by a boy, not quite of age. Two little faces peeked out from behind him.

"Get outta here," said the boy, giving each little kid a shove.

"Gunnar. Do not push your siblings." A woman had appeared at the door — Lady Hilda Maedoer Holding, Spirit of the Raven. Mr Holding must already be at the palace for work.

"Best day, Miss Ella. Thank you for coming." Hilda was older than Ella, but younger than her parents. She was dressed in a comfy elvish tunic, but something about the way she carried herself was intimidating. Her dark hair was pulled back into a severe bun, and only a few straight tendrils framed her face. They hung there like they dare not move.

While Hilda Holding looked well put together and stood with authority before the others in the room, she seemed unsure of how to begin interviewing a nanny.

"What do your children like to do for fun?" Ella asked.

Hilda looked relieved for the question. "Andri and Kristin love to just play with their toys when they get home from school. And with Gunnar…" her voice lowered, "I usually just send him outside to play with his friends."

"We don't play, Mom." Gunnar scowled. "We fight."

"Right. Sorry." Hilda looked at Ella and shrugged.

"Glima?" Ella asked Gunnar directly.

"Yeah," said Gunnar. "I'm going for the belt as soon as I'm allowed, so I have to practice. Dad says I can't fight at Marilla's until I come of age."

"So you've got a few years to practice," said Ella.

Gunnar rolled his eyes. Ella watched as he pulled a board out from behind the door. He threw it toward the ground and charmed it before it touched. Then he jumped upon the hovering slab and left out the open front door.

"Wasteworthy." Hilda closed the door behind him. Ella could tell that Hilda didn't approve of Gunnar using his energy on a hoverboard. Still, Ella thought it looked fun — just the thing for a growing lad-elf.

Ella and Hilda got along well. Hilda invited Ella to stay for tea all the while conducting Ella's nanny interview. Hilda confirmed that she and her husband were both Palace Advisors who were rarely home. They were looking for a nanny for the early morning as well as the late, second half of the day when the wee ones were out of school. Gunnar Becklin Holding, Spirit of the Wind, their oldest child was sixty-seven, or twelve in human years. He had two siblings: Andri Payne Holding, Spirit of the Trees was twenty-seven, or five in human years, and Kristin Payj Holding, Spirit of the Ocean was only sixteen, or three in human years. Their family was very unusual, as elvish couples usually only had one child. It was always a wild surprise when nature blessed a family with a second child.

Three was unheard of, something from Alveland storybooks.

Elves who have more than one child are rumored to be descendants of the strong, long-suffering Princess Kari. According to such history, one would think that perhaps Hilda Holding could be of royal blood, which of course is why she held the title of Lady Hilda Holding. Ella would certainly have a lot of work for herself if she accepted this nanny job.

Ella had been nervous when she arrived but was not any more. After her interview, she felt confident. This interview was nothing like the ones she had to endure yesterday. She hoped Lady Hilda liked her, because after this nanny job, she was completely out of ideas and would have to return home a failure. If it was this hard to pay for housing, how hard was it going to be to save Megs? Ella didn't even want to know.

———

Ella was embarrassed to find only one wooden desk left in the classroom when she arrived at her first class, five minutes tardy. Her teacher would surely realize that she was the late, unorganized student. Not that she cared. She was only here because she had to be. She didn't notice Oliver at first, not until she felt his glare on her. What was he even doing in here, anyway?

Ella sat at the empty desk and tucked her puffy skirts beneath her so she would fit. She was wearing one of her favorite dresses — navy blue with rhinestones on the bodice. The rhinestones were sewn to match the star pattern in mid-June during the Summer Solstice. Underneath the dress, she had tied both of the petticoats she had brought with her to University — one less than normal. It didn't seem practical to bring three, it would have taken up far too much space in her trunks.

"Good morning." Oliver planted himself in the front of the room and rubbed his hands together. He was dressed for Hunting duties — pants made of a thick material and thick-soled boots. His tunic was short with a V-neck. It had no embroidery. Ella could see that underneath the V of his shirt were some well-defined and deeply tanned muscles.

Sitting in such close proximity to Oliver, Ella caught his scent. He smelled like the wind as it blew in from the ocean. Ella had always found the ocean breeze a comforting smell. However, she felt no comfort in Oliver's presence. Especially not after he had saved her life again.

"Oliver Agnarsson, Spirit of the Ocean. I'm here at the Commander's request. Prepare for lecture one."

Ella supposed it made sense that he smelled like the ocean since he was an ocean Spirit. She assumed that her scent was floral in nature.

What she couldn't believe was that Oliver was her teacher. She didn't want to take classes, but it was one of Commander Agnarsson's conditions for allowing her to accompany the retrieval team. She didn't want to take classes, and she didn't want to be a Huntress. She wanted to find Megs. She would never be able to take Oliver seriously. The other students shuffled a paper or a pad onto their writing desks, but not Ella. How was she supposed to know what she needed for class? She hadn't taken a class in a hundred years. And she also had never been one to take notes.

Oliver began his lecture.

"Let us begin with announcements." He paced the room, eventually coming close to her desk. When he arrived at Ella's desk he frowned. Ella suddenly wanted to be invisible. Maybe he wouldn't notice that she hadn't brought any materials to class. She hoped he wouldn't glare at her any more. And she hoped he wouldn't notice that she hadn't brought any materials to class. She tucked her curls behind her ears and stared at her desk as though something were on it. Slowly, he returned to his own desk, retrieved a bit of parchment along with a quill and placed it in front of Ella. She felt her cheeks flush.

"Announcement one: the Shadow update. The Hunters believe the Shadow is heading north-east toward the Far Lands, but moving slowly. The Hunters believe it is regrouping and deciding where it should attack next. As you know, it is attracted to power and that is why it has attacked the Palace Province several times. You also may have heard that the Hunters believe the Wicked Three are behind the Shadow itself."

A stillness crept over the room after Oliver mentioned the Wicked Three. He cleared his throat and continued.

"The attack team is tracking the Shadow. Home team is repairing Alveland and offering aid to families of the Missing. The retrieval team is looking for leads. Unfortunately, most of the information is from past attacks, not the current one. No travel for any of the three teams is scheduled as of right now."

Oliver threw his notes on his desk and continued pacing with his hands clasped behind his back.

Ella looked around the room. Her notepaper looked different from the other students' notepapers. When the parchment was placed in front of her, she immediately began to doodle. She doodled her favorite Alveland flowers, ShaSha and Dietz. Then, she doodled a picture of the fern flower to match the one on her long necklace from Megs. The other students furiously scratched down Oliver's words. Then again, these were all elves who were aspiring to be Hunters. It was ironic that Ella had to take classes because of Megs, since Megs didn't believe in organized institutions.

"Announcement two," said Oliver. "Thirty new Hunters are being trained at University currently. Well, thirty-one." Oliver turned so he could frown at Ella. "If you graduate before the Shadow returns or one of the teams depart, you may be added to a team. Regardless, after graduation you will be assigned a post. The post may be in the Palace Province, but it may be at one of the other three locations."

"Announcement three: be prepared for Total Exertion training at some point during your time at University. Each elf must practice Total Exertion once in a controlled environment so the Hunters can see how far their energy reaches, and how long it takes to recover."

Ella knew it was time to go when the other students began packing up their things. She tucked her doodle parchment in her bag and quietly placed the quill back on Oliver's desk.

"Come prepared for class tomorrow." His low voice seemed to rumble across the very stones in the floor.

"I didn't know you were teaching," Ella said.

"Neither did I." Oliver didn't bother to hide the bitterness in his voice. He replaced his quill, slung his Hunterpack across his back and left the room before Ella.

Tomorrow she'd bring her own parchment and quill.

Her first class hadn't gone well. Commander Agnarsson said she had to attend classes. He didn't say she had to take notes or pay attention. Ella retreated to the Amarind Building — her new home. Her room was up one flight of stairs. When she arrived, the door was slightly ajar. Ella had to duck under a lady-elf who was standing on a chair and lighting the wall sconces with her hands. Haven, Ella's mystery room-mate, had finally arrived last night. She was a Hunteress who had been on another assignment, traveling independently and was finally meeting up with the larger group of Hunters.

If possible, Haven Archef Rae, Spirit of the Sun, was even more famous than Oliver. With flaming red hair that she allowed to extend into a curly orb around her head, Haven could stop a lad-elf in his tracks simply by applying lipstick. And on top of her looks, she knew six ways to kill an elf with her feet on the ground. More if she were allowed to jump, swim or wield a weapon. In fact, Haven held the same Hunting rank as Oliver: General. There were four of them, total, in all of Alveland. Haven was General of the Netherelves Quad, located in the North Mountains.

Ella had heard the stories, and she knew that Haven had been born and raised as a Princess of the Netherelves. Having lived in the mountains their whole lives, Netherelves had an incredible tolerance for the cold. Tolerance? They loved it. How she escaped her royal duties and became a Hunteress, Ella did not know.

Ella glanced around the room and decided that she felt at home. Ella also felt frustrated by the Hunter's unknown timeline. She hoped, though, for Megs' sake, that the retrieval team would leave sooner rather than later. She palmed the bottom of a string of firefly lights which she had hung above her bed. One by one, her fire slid up the strand and lit each charmed firefly as it passed, leaving behind a warm glow. When she had arrived the night before, Haven had painted the walls eggshell, and left the back wall exposed stone. She added two cushioned bed headboards which leaned against the stone. Floor to ceiling windows let in a dreamy amount of sunlight.

"Best day," said Haven.

"Best day." Ella flushed, still feeling a little awestruck around Haven. Ella laid her school bag down on her bed.

"I hope the headboards and sconces are to your liking," Haven said.

"Are you kidding? They're beautiful," Ella said.

Haven smiled.

"Are my firefly lights okay?"

"Perfect," Haven said. "The laundry monster could go, though."

Ella looked over at her growing pile of soiled elvish linens and blushed. She had never had to deal with her own laundry before — another thing Mitsy had always taken care of. Ella would figure out how to take care of it. She would. Maybe after she took care of the pile of unread class materials that lay on her desk from class this morning.

"I teach this morning, but would you like to meet for tea in town, later?" Haven asked.

"Of course." Ella liked tea, but concern filled her thoughts about her growing piles of responsibilities that she didn't know how to deal with. The Commander had asked Haven if she'd teach Human Relations. It was a subject about which Haven was passionate, so of course she agreed. On her most recent assignment, Haven had been stationed inside the human realm for several months.

She was supposed to find out the truth about an Alveland rumor. The rumor stated that one of the Wicked Three was creating a domain in the human realm. She was stationed near one of the portals in North America, waiting for some clues or indication, but none ever came. When the Shadow attacked the Palace Province, Haven was called to Alveland instead.

Ella reached under her pillow and pulled out her sleeping chameleon. Ella unloaded a pile of kale and hibiscus flowers on her end table. "Picked these for you." ShaSha looked very excited. Well, he looked as excited as a chameleon can look. Admittedly slowly, he walked over to the end table without expression on his face. But Ella knew that he was excited, anyway.

"Has ShaSha been hiding from Blair all day?" Ella asked.

"Pretty much." Blair was Haven's tzi, a field mouse with flair. Somehow, she seemed to have pink tinted fur. Haven swears she didn't charm it.

Ella was not concerned about the two tzis hurting each other. No, after all, they were both bonded animals. However, ShaSha tended to be antisocial, so a pink furred mouse probably frightened her.

"Have you seen Dietze?" Ella asked.

"Megs' tzi?" Haven shook her head.

"She may have gone back to Megs' house to wait for her. I'll stop by to feed her when we meet for tea."

Ella picked up her day satchel.

"Where are you going?" Haven asked.

"My nanny job," Ella said.

"Good luck."

Haven had no idea.

Ella stood, staring at the flickering sconce in the foyer of the Holding residence. It was an oddly peaceful monument in this chaotic habitat. She had been a nanny for three hours and she was covered in pie batter. Scratch that, everything was covered in pie batter. Every bit of the Holding residence was white — or it used to be — from the washed wooden walls to the stone floors and countertops, it was all white. And Ella could still see some of it peeping through smears of dough.

Ella had not escaped the pie-plosion, either. Her curls escaped from her bun, though, and frizzed almost audibly around her face. She was breathing heavily and silently praying for a break. Kristin and Andri, in all of their childish glory, had been helping her make dinner. Like hell.

Ella just wanted to make a seafood pie. How hard could that be?

How hard indeed.

At first, Ella had invited Kristin to stand on a stool to knead the pre-made batter into a smooth dough, which she started out doing quite successfully. Then, she allowed Andri to shuck corn. When Ella realized she needed to add eggs to the pie, she left the room to retrieve them from the underground cellar. That was her critical mistake. When she returned, Andri had stolen the batter from Kristin and was racing around the kitchen with it. He had the bowl extended overhead while Kristin chased after. When Kristin got too close, Andri used the batter as ammunition to keep her away. Both children's hands were sticky with half-mixed batter.

That wasn't even the biggest cause of the mess. When Ella tried to wrangle the children, the batter smeared on her clothes. She had grabbed Andri around the waist, but Kristin snatched the bowl from him and escaped around the kitchen island and down the hallway, leaving slippery footprints in her wake. That was discouraging, but what really started the olive colored energy of discouragement to radiate from Ella was when she let go of Andri to follow Kristin, he knocked into the island and spilled the bowl of broth and vegetables onto the floor.

And by the Spirits, God only knew Gunnar's whereabouts. Ella sat down in the foyer and rested her head on a square of skin along her arm that wasn't sticky. Well, she thought it wasn't sticky. Now she probably had batter on her forehead. When she had arrived at the Holding's at two, Mrs Holding was dressed for her Advisor Summit, preparing to meet her husband for their afternoon meeting with the King. She had just sat the children at the table with a bowl of snack nuts, and they sat there innocently munching until Hilda left, walked down the road and crossed the Fainde River Bridge, out of sight. At that point, Gunnar shouldered Vex, his Slow

Loris and exploded out the front door on his hoverboard, leaving it open behind him. That was hours ago, and she hadn't heard from him since. Ella had sent him a sound message, but of course, he hadn't responded.

She was messing this up. How could an elf mess up a nanny job? Weren't wee ones supposed to be little blessings? Ella plugged her ears to give herself a momentary reprieve from the screaming. Hilda assured her that if all three children were alive at the end of each day, then she was doing her job. But Ella took no comfort.

Hilda obviously knew that her children were difficult, but this did not deter Ella from wanting to provide them with a functional home with structure and love. She decided, standing there in the foyer, that these children were now, in part, hers. And by the Spirits she was going to care for them. However, her efforts toward functional, structured and loving were currently being spurned by chaos, anger and frustration.

There was a knock at the front door which Ella heard only because she was standing next to it. Hopefully it was Gunnar. If it was either of the Advisor Holdings, she'd be in trouble, and possibly unemployed. One of their children was missing, and the rest of their family and belongings were covered in pie batter.

To Ella's unpleasant surprise, Oliver stood on the Holding's doorstep. His athletic form cast a shadow over her in the evening sunshine.

"What are you doing here?" asked Ella.

"I heard screaming."

Oliver palmed a wolf cane at his side. If she weren't so frustrated, she would have been amused by the fact that her children had brought an armed Hunter to her door.

"It's just the wees," Ella assured him. Oliver put away the wolf cane.

Oliver's gaze followed the many trails of pie batter across her clothing. "Look at you," he said. The corners of his mouth twitched upward.

"You may not," said Ella. "You who never smile are not allowed to smirk at my appearance."

"I smile," said Oliver.

Ella gave him a deadpan look.

"Only when it's necessary."

Just then, two squealing blurs smeared their way through the foyer. Oliver, quick as summer lightning, reached over the top of the children and extricated the bowl from Andri's hands.

"How in Alveland did you do that?" asked Ella.

Oliver shrugged.

Andri and Kristin continued to chase each other out of the room, even without the bowl.

"Are you quite all right?" Oliver asked. "You look unwell."

"I'm well," said Ella. "Kind of well. I just need—" What did she just need? She couldn't quit her job or she couldn't pay for her housing. And if she couldn't pay for her housing, she couldn't look for Megs. She'd end up in her parents' home with Mitsy bringing her tea, no best friend and nothing to do with herself.

Oliver raised an eyebrow. "Shall I help?"

"Maybe." Ella did not want help. She was done being rescued. And she especially didn't want Oliver's help. However, the amount of batter that was all over the house rather than baked and in the children's bellies was troubling. Not to mention that she had no idea where Gunnar actually was.

Oliver entered the foyer and leaned his tall frame against the door frame. He was far too close for comfort. Ella could feel heat and energy radiating from him. She definitely felt his normal, black energy, full of annoyance, but others as well. "I'll read the wees a story. You make dinner."

"You think they'll listen to a story?" Had Oliver just told her what to do?

Ella led Oliver into the Holding's study. Floor to ceiling windows let in evening light which illuminated their two walls of books. He perused until he chose two picture books.

Ella crossed her arms in the study and watched in shock as he called to the wee littles.

Like men to the sirens the two wee ones barreled into the foyer and attached themselves to Oliver's legs.

What in Alveland was happening? Was Oliver a better nanny than she? Ella decided not to ask. She gripped the batter bowl tightly and backed slowly into the kitchen, hoping to escape unnoticed. Setting the bowl on the counter, she finger combed her knotty hair and twisted it to the side. Oh, how her hair needed Mitsy. Next, she wet a towel and scrubbed the large patches of stickiness off of her skin and clothes. Better.

The only reason they had batter to begin with was because Hilda Holding had assembled it ahead of time as well as what went inside. Ella had never prepared food of any kind in her life — Mitsy or Cook had always done it for her and her family. She rolled out the remainder of the pie crust and assembled the dinner pie. Once it was in the oven, she stood very still in the kitchen. It was quiet. She flattened herself against the wall and peeked quickly through the doorway where she saw Oliver reading an ever-growing tower of books to the two sticky children. Kristin was sucking on her finger which probably tasted like batter. Andri held tightly to his favorite blanket. Ella's heart did a flip-flop. This was all very cute. And confusing.

The front door slammed and Ella heard grumpy footsteps stomping toward the kitchen.

"Is dinner ready?"

Ella immediately felt her mom-throb headache, only her mother was nowhere near. Apparently, Gunnar could bring forth a mom-throb as well. "Hello Gunnar. It's nice to see you. Dinner is in the oven and will be ready shortly."

Gunnar rolled his eyes and tried to run upstairs to the safety of his room. Unfortunately, he almost ran over Oliver and his siblings.

"Hey!" he said. He readied himself for a verbal attack about his siblings being underfoot until he saw who was in his foyer.

"No freaking way."

"Don't say freaking in front of your siblings," said Ella. "This is my... er... friend..."

"Oliver Agnarsson, Spirit of the Ocean," breathed Gunnar.

"Pleased to meet you." Oliver extended his hand and Gunnar shook it, jaw agape.

"But you're in my house," said Gunnar.

"I am," said Oliver. The corners of his mouth twitched upward for the second time this visit.

"What are you doing in my house? I mean, it's very great that you're in my house, but... What I mean is..."

"I heard screaming," said Oliver.

"Are you staying for dinner?" Gunnar asked.

Dear Alveland, no. He couldn't possibly stay for dinner. He came here on his own, so she certainly didn't owe him dinner. Granted, she didn't kick him out, either, but she definitely didn't ask him to stay. It's not like any reading he did could make up for the past.

"If I'm invited," Oliver said.

Ella couldn't not invite him, now that he had helped her babysit the wee ones.

"Of course, you're invited." Ella hoped she hid the grudge in her voice as she turned to set an extra place at the table.

Chapter 15

Attack Team

Thursday, September 6, 1899

Because of the new moon, starless night, Oliver relied heavily on his elvish vision as he ran through the chilled night air away from town. The dew on the grass thickened as he raced toward the foothills. He hoped he wouldn't be late. Not that he had been invited to the meeting, but he was going anyway. Oliver began to run.

It had been a terrible morning. His father had assigned him to teach one of the new Hunter classes, and this was his first day. Ella had been there, of course, tormenting him with her flakiness and sweet honeysuckle scent. She should not be a Huntress. And somehow, the things that drove him craziest about her, drove him crazy. That didn't even make sense — it was time to focus on Hunting as he always did. Oliver knew the attack team had been out tracking the Shadow this morning, which is where he should have been, rather than in the classroom.

Oliver ran past the Highland Elvish dwellings and continued down the footpath until he came to a cave. A warm glow emanated from it and hushed voices hovered just out of understanding. Not wanting to startle his teammates, Oliver picked up a rock and tapped the Hunter's secret knock on the walls of the cave — three slow taps. Three slow taps returned. Oliver tapped back two more taps which were met with a 'ha', from one of the others.

"Oliver Agnarsson," Oliver announced himself so he didn't get a fireball to the chest or a charm to the head. He saw a small, welcoming fire flickering in the back of the small cave surrounded by eight other Hunters. They were the attack team — his team. Most had a warm greeting for him, as they were used to his presence and even leadership at these meetings. He nodded in acknowledgement. The only person who didn't greet him warmly was Celvin. Celvin was jealous of Oliver's fame and rank which was stupid. Oliver didn't hunt for the fame and rank. He did it because he had to. He was a Hunter — plain and simple. The rank came with each consecutive success. Some say it was because of his father's rank, but if anything, his father made it harder on him than anyone else.

"I'm leading this meeting." Celvin stood.

"Lead away." Oliver dropped his Hunterpack on the ground and sat on an unoccupied boulder next to the fire.

"Maps," said Celvin.

Lindy, a lady-elf, stood and unrolled a large bit of parchment. "Bulkrum, Fangrii and I sent out our energy search from these points here, here and here." She pointed to the map. "The Shadow flees north. The energy is nigh undetectable, retreating, but not gone. Karii sent her bird's eye search. None have contradictory reports. Shadow traveling north at seventeen knots."

"Why?" Celvin asked.

Lindy shrugged.

"So we either pursue and continue to try a prediction, or we let it go and turn our efforts to long-term fight tactics while remaining here." Celvin was thinking out loud.

No one disagreed with his accurate analysis of the situation.

By Alveland, they had to go. If there was any chance of them catching the Shadow off-guard and actually locating what was at its source, they had to go. It was imperative. And he would sure as hell be on their ship when they left.

"Reasons to go." Celvin prompted his team.

"Obviously, the Shadow could be retreating. If it's really weakening, then we would be remiss not to follow and attack, now," Lindy said.

"But if it's not retreating, then we attack on water where Land Spirit Elves have fewer resources, we use up our rations and miss an opportunity to recuperate, all for what?"

Several attack team members nodded as they continued to look into the flickering fire. Oliver didn't have to worry about land resources, he was an ocean Spirit. He would extract just as much energy for magic and survival out at sea as he would on land, maybe even more so. However, if his team was at a disadvantage, he would be, too.

"I say we go," Celvin said finally.

Oliver silently cheered. Should he tell his dad he was resigning from his training position, or let him figure it out from his absence? All those years he was left to figure things out on his own left him thinking he would leave it up to deduction.

"Any other business?" Celvin stood to close the meeting.

Oliver stood. He wasn't looking forward to this part. There was no easy way to do this, so he was just going to attack it — like the attack elf he was. "I'd like to come."

"No." Celvin answered so quickly, Oliver had barely even gotten the question out.

Oliver crossed his arms over his chest. It was only a matter of time before the rest of the team came to his aid. This was his team, not Celvin's.

"He'd only help us," Lindy said.

"He doesn't belong on the retrieval team," Bulkrum said.

"I'm not going against the Commander's orders. He stays," Celvin said.

Celvin's words meant nothing to him. He'd be on that ship, no matter what.

Chapter 16

High Ropes

Thursday, October 6, 1899

Ella kept tugging at her shirt, trying to get more coverage out of the ridiculous outfit she was wearing. This wasn't even taking into consideration the pair of mandatory Hunter boots. They were the most hideous things she had ever seen. They were black and synthetic with thick, clunky soles. They were entirely unnecessary for any situation, in her opinion. She was also wearing linen lad-elf pants and a fitted shirt that was supposed to avoid getting stuck on her harness. And why would she need a harness? Because they were undergoing physical training for their Huntership today. Ella didn't even want a Huntership. She just wanted to find Megs.

Ella stood on a platform attached to one of the high birches at the edge of the forest. The Hunters had constructed this rope course in the quaint, forest-lined meadow by the University. Ella found it peaceful, or at least she did before it was turned into a training course. She used to come and lean against their comforting bark and read. And when she was upset, she could send her difficult energies into the trunks and they would pull her burden far from her, sending it into the earth. Obviously, the Hunters had not done anything to truly injure any of the forest — they were still elves after all. But now ropes and ladders, lines and pulleys blocked easy access to the trees.

The Hunters had a motto about pushing themselves to their limits in order to preserve their glorious strength. It was supposed to help them survive anything — from squalls to sieges. Certainly, if Alveland were ever under attack she wouldn't be called upon to fight. No, they would call upon the real Hunters, not her. So why in Alveland was she being asked to participate in these cursed physical training? It was bad enough enduring Oliver's boring lectures every day.

Not to mention that she was re-wearing her lad-elf pants from an earlier physical training session in the week. If she was really ready to admit it, she was re-wearing the same pants she had used for every physical training session so far. They had not smelled fresh when she put them on, but she had not had time to launder her clothing. Had she figured out how to launder her clothing yet? Nope. Ella wanted Mitsy.

There were three other elves on the platform with her, one being Haven who looked completely comfortable in her Huntress garb. Comfortable and yet somehow also ruggedly beautiful. Her orb of fiery red hair was tied behind her in a jolly puff where it would, no doubt, be out of her way for training. She was leaning over the railing and flirting with a lad-elf named Hawi. Hawi Traler Landek, Spirit of Sky, was a new Hunter recruit like Ella, though Ella had never spoken with him.

Another elf on the platform was Mr Grumpier-than-a-mountain-lion, himself, Oliver. He was just about to demonstrate their course. Ella rolled her eyes as Oliver stepped off the platform and began his climb. He quickly made his way across the terrifyingly skinny rope bridge to the next platform. Then, he switched his belay and climbed to the top of the next tree. He ziplined across the field to a third platform. Here, he jumped down into a murky pond and scaled a hill, set with bars for stability. He then successfully went down the other side.

Even from a distance, Ella could see his arm muscles rippling as he moved. He really was a golden statue specimen — even for an elf. His last task was to use the pulley system to hike himself back to his original platform.

When he returned, Oliver was barely even breathing heavily. How was she supposed to do any of that? She was trained only for Royal Elvish Tea. This was unfair. This was cruelty to royals. Well, she wasn't a royal any more. But it was still cruel. Oliver commanded everyone to pair up with a belay partner as he removed his harnesses. Haven agreed to be partners with the cute, new recruit, which left Ella without a partner. That was fine with her, maybe she'd get out of participating.

She watched Haven and her partner scoot across the rope bridge. Several other elves left their platforms to begin the course as well. Ella leaned against the tree trunk feeling its cool, smooth bark on her back where her shirt was slightly lifted above the waist of her pants.

The second set of elves left the platform. Oliver milled around calling out orders to pairs who were stuck. The pair in the murky pool was having a hard time gripping the hill after submerging in the slimy water.

No, thank you. She scooted behind the tree and waited for the second pair of elves to finish. There was a large group of sweaty, muddy elves surrounding Oliver as they finished with the course. Ella quietly tip-toed down the rope ladder along the back of the birch. She was close to getting out of this.

"It's important to be well prepared and continually stay physically trained because in a real-life situation, the elements won't necessarily be so controlled and predictable," Oliver explained. "Grabbing onto rocks as one falls down a mountain is a lot more difficult than scaling the back side of a hill with bars. Next physical training will be with combatants. You're all dismissed."

The elves turned to leave, Ella with them, being sure to slip into the crowd so as not to be seen in her clean clothes. She was about to reach the fence at the edge of the field that led back into the University building property when she felt a strong hand on her shoulder. She turned slowly to see Oliver's scowl.

"I didn't have a partner," Ella said.

Oliver glowered at her. She let her shoulders droop as she returned to the birch tree and ascended it once again.

To her horror, Oliver followed her up. She was very aware of her backside being so close to him. Surely, he wasn't going to be her partner. No, if she had to clear this course, she would complete it on her own.

Oliver helped her into her harness first, then donned his own, making sure to fasten it over his Hunterpack. Ella stepped out onto the rope ladder and began to slide her feet across. Gripping the rope reminded her of the rope swing at the Fainde River. She loved that swing. She did not love this rope ladder. Oliver followed her along, unmistakably playing the role of her partner. She was nearly to the next platform when she accidentally put her hand on a friendly gecko who was curiously traveling along the rope railing.

Ella squealed and jerked her hand away. She lost her balance and grabbed for the rope as she fell. Unfortunately, the rope was out of reach, and the thing that she grabbed onto just happened to be Oliver's leg. She pulled him down, too. Both elves swung below the rope bridge from their belays.

Ella was suddenly glad of her dreaded waist harness. When their flailing slowed, they hung next to each other and Oliver glared at Ella. It wasn't like she grabbed him on purpose.

"What in Alveland were you thinking?" Oliver asked.

"Me? This is your fault." Ella shoved Oliver away from her.

"You yanked me off the rope bridge." Oliver came crashing back towards her, holding out his hand to her rope to try to avoid hurting her.

"You made me do this stupid rope course," said Ella. She shoved him again.

"All Hunters in training do it." Oliver shoved her rope.

"I'm not a Hunter in training — thank the Spirits — I just want Megs." She shoved again.

"You're not going to find Megs." Oliver finally shoved Ella's rope.

Oliver's shove was gentle, but his words had slapped her across the face. Ella looked into the forest and blinked back tears.

"I'll fix this," Oliver spoke quietly into the awkward silence. He must have noticed that his words had injured her. When she looked at him, a look of pity was on his face before he rearranged it into his normal Oliver-scowl. He grabbed onto his own belay rope and began to climb with an incredible display of strength, one hand over the next. "Damnit."

"What's wrong?" Ella asked.

"Your rope is tangled up with mine. I can't climb any higher without untwisting it, and I can't quite reach the bridge, yet." Oliver lunged for the bridge but fell short. Soon he was dangling from his belay rope once again. Next, Ella watched as he swung himself closer to the bridge and stuck his foot out to try to grab it. That attempt was also unsuccessful. As he swung slower and slower, he wrapped his arms around her to steady himself.

Ella looked down at his arms wrapped around her waist. Heat spread throughout her body, starting from where his hands gripped her and spreading up to her cheeks. Oliver quickly let go which caused him to dangle out of control again.

Without any choice, they grabbed onto each other to find steadiness.

"I have an extra rope in my Hunterpack," Oliver said. "You'll have to get it out, but then I can loop the rope bridge and pull us up."

Ella reached over his shoulder which brought their faces extremely close. Once again she breathed in more of Oliver's oceany scent. She paused in her search for the rope long enough to get her inner energy under control. She felt across his strong shoulders and into the Hunterpack where she did, indeed, feel a coil of rope.

"Keep me stable," Oliver said.

Ella held onto him while he looped one end of the rope to his waist harness. His lad-elf shirt lifted and she could see strong, sculpted muscles beneath. Oliver flung the other end of his rope coil toward the bridge. Unfortunately, the middle section had wound its way around Ella's ankle. Without its full length available, the rope didn't reach its intended destination. It dropped like a dead snake toward the ground, some twelve feet below the two stranded elves.

Ella began to pull the rope up, in the process, wrapping it further around herself and Oliver. Maybe she and Oliver should use their magic to get themselves to safety. It would take a wasteworthy amount of energy, but it would end this entanglement.

"Just stop." Oliver grabbed her arms, ceasing the movement of the rope. His face was red and a vein pulsed across his neck. Angry ripples of energy rolled off him, gray and dangerous. Ella dropped the rope from her hands. If possible, it wound itself into further tangles around their feet.

Someone cleared their throat from near the birch tree. Oliver rolled his eyes so far back into his head they were almost invisible. He really didn't get along with his pa. Ella felt the slightest bit of pity for him, thinking about her own doting father. Tension between Oliver and the Commander had been there for as long as Ella could remember. Ella began to remember her pity for Oliver that she felt when he was a lonely wee one. Ella shook off the notion. Oliver didn't need her pity. Only a month ago he had saved her and everyone else in Alveland.

"I couldn't help but notice..." Commander Agnarsson's voice trailed off in a sarcastic cadence.

Oliver growled quietly like an animal. "We've got it," Oliver said.

"Really?" the Commander asked.

"We'll use magic if we have to," Oliver said.

"Ridiculous choice," the Commander said. "Wasteworthy."

Oliver muttered under his breath.

"Commander, we could use a helping hand." Ella scowled at Oliver.

Ella felt relieved that the Commander was available to help, but Oliver seemed to stop breathing altogether.

The Commander ascended the ladder into the birch and easily pulled them toward the tree. Once Ella was on the ladder, Oliver was able to, with much problem solving, unwind the rope from Ella's waist and legs.

More heat radiated through her body. Get control of yourself, she scolded. The turquoise energy of embarrassment began to roll off her. If she wasn't careful, the maroon energy of desire would mix in. She wouldn't be able to control it if it got too strong. And if Oliver ever noticed, she'd have to move to the mountains and become a Netherelf where she would immediately freeze into an ice nugget. Oliver was Emil's best friend, she reminded herself. And he was Oliver. She thought of Emil, who she used to be engaged to. While humans were uncouth, powerless and odd, Ella had heard that even they knew the 'no best friends' rule.

Once her ropes were free she quickly scurried up the ladder to thank the Commander.

"I'll be interested to know your training evaluation," Commander Agnarsson said. "Have I made an unwise exception?"

Ella felt her face blush. He wasn't wrong about her. She had no business in Hunter training. Oliver certainly wouldn't give her a glowing report. She still maintained that she didn't want to become a Hunter. She wanted to find Megs. However, she thought it unwise to explain this reasoning to the Commander.

Oliver ascended the ladder next and alighted the platform with a smirk of pleasure now that Ella was in trouble. He was infuriating. He was also in charge of her training evaluation.

Ella chose her least-offensive smelling, linen elvish tunic from her pile of dirty clothes. If only she knew how to launder her linens. She could also use a lesson on clean hair. She had taken out all the updo pins, and let it fall. Now, however, she was all tangles and frizz like a forest animal. She tried to comb her brush through it, but it got stuck. She tied a silken scarf around her head in hopes of hiding the snarls and the brush.

Her make-up wasn't exactly faring well, either. Though she had scrubbed her face with soap, the last remnants of make-up refused to come off. This morning, she had finally thrown a towel over her mirror so she wouldn't have to deal with her reflection. She caught a glimpse of herself in the window of her dorm, though and she thought she resembled a blushing raccoon.

When Ella sat down in the dimly lit classroom, surrounded by wooden desks, she noticed Oliver's gaze lingering on her for just a moment longer than he should have. He, too, must think she looked disgusting.

She couldn't do this anymore.

She needed help.

She needed Mitsy.

She needed a clean updo and laundered clothes that didn't smell like yesterday's cafeteria dinner. Speaking of dinner, she also needed food. She had missed breakfast because she had slept too late. If she'd have tried to go to the cafeteria when she woke up, she would have missed class. She'd opened the refrigerator and found eggs, which would have made a fine breakfast, except she certainly didn't know how to cook an egg. Cook had always taken care of that. A tear trickled down her cheek and splattered on her notebook. Maybe she had left home too soon.

Oliver began his lecture on mapping, something the retrieval team used all the time. Another tear trickled down Ella's cheek. She was supposed to have been Alveland's Princess. And eventually the Queen. Was she also bringing shame on Emil as she struggled to care of her appearance? Alveland's almost-Princess was in shambles. She didn't look like someone a Prince should be engaged to.

Ella sniffed and wiped at her eyes. Without stopping his lecture, Oliver passed her his handkerchief. When she took it, she excused herself from the class, surely never to go back.

Where should she go? Should she turn herself in as a failure and go home?

No. Not yet, at least.

The day she turned up at home was the day she dubbed herself a total life failure. She clutched her notebook to her chest and walked as fast as she could back to her room. She collapsed into her bed in a pile of frizz and tears.

Before long, Ella felt a hand on her back. "You don't look so good, Roomie."

She kicked off the bed covers, upset the tea and stomped over to her mirror. She took in her appearance. Her hair could have been mistaken for a rodent's nest. The bags under her eyes were big enough to pack for a trip. Her skin was sallow and her lips almost pale enough to match her skin.

"Come on," Haven gave her a hand up. "First thing's first. Shampoo and a curl pick." Haven walked to her own dresser and handed them to Ella.

"What?" Ella sat up.

"Anyone can see that you could use a hand, Roomie. You may know how to be a Princess, but you do not know how to be a normal, lady-elf."

Ella followed Haven down the hall to the bathroom. Haven guided Ella to the dragon-footed, porcelain tub. In the sconce light, Haven helped Ella stick her head under the tub faucet and work a good lather into her hair. Her arms got tired. Mitsy always did this. Ella rinsed, and then did another shampoo under Haven's direction.

Just taking care of Ella's hair took many time-consuming steps. Haven squirted a bunch of conditioner into her hand and told her to work it into her hair, starting near her scalp and ending — feet below — at the tips of her blonde curls. It squished between her fingers and made her hair feel slippery and healthy. Once she rinsed that out, Haven handed her something small and pointy that looked like a weapon. It was a curl pick, and you used it the opposite way you use conditioner: from the tips to the scalp. Ella slowly and gently pulled out the furious tangles that had embedded themselves in her hair over the past week. Haven helped. It was painful. When they were done, Ella was able to run her fingers all the way through her hair with ease.

"You know what?" Haven said. "I'm going to cut some length off, so you have less to deal with."

"No, no. I couldn't possibly cut my hair short."

"Relax, Blondie. Yes, I'm going to cut it. But it won't be short."

Ella fussed while Haven hacked off a foot of hair. The ends now rested just above her elbows instead of far below her bottom. She suddenly felt light and breezy.

"Now to the sink," said Haven pointing the way across the spacious, stone bathroom.

"What's at the sink?" Ella asked.

Haven handed her a bottle of oily liquid and a cotton ball. Apparently, you need special stuff called witch hazel and oil to scrub the face color off. After several long minutes, Ella no longer had raccoon eyes. When she finished drying her face off, she looked in the mirror.

"Better?" asked Haven.

"Better," Ella sighed.

"Next stop: the laundry room."

"Oh thank the Spirits," Ella said. She could not stand to re-wear one more dirty tunic.

One hour later, Ella had a basket full of clean clothing to hang dry outside their room window.

"Now that your hair is dry," said Haven. "Let's work on fixing it and applying make-up."

"On myself?" asked Ella.

"That's how normal people do it, Blondie."

Ella looked at Haven's beautiful coif and decided to do whatever she said. An hour later, Ella could put her hair in a ponytail, a half ponytail and a simple braid. She learned how to brush mascara on her eyelashes and lipstick on her lips. Haven said she was not ready for anything else.

"Thank you," said Ella.

Haven nodded.

"Haven?"

"Yes?"

"Now that I am adept at personal hygiene, can you teach me how to make some food? I'm soooo hungry."

Ella stood at the precipice of the ocean cliffs, leaning way out over the churning sea. She breathed in deeply as the ocean breeze whipped through her freshly trimmed, washed and detangled hair. Ella felt like she had conquered the world. She could clean and care for her hair. She could fix it. She could apply and remove make-up. She could launder clothing. And she could cook food for herself. She felt as though nothing was stopping her. In fact, finding Megs didn't seem like such a far-fetched idea. No, Ella decided right there on those ocean cliffs that she would be the best damn Huntress the Palace Province had ever seen. (Except Haven, of course.) She would become a Huntress capable of finding a beloved elf. And she would become worthy of her fern flower nomination.

After dinner, Haven took Ella to Marilla's to celebrate. Ella wore one of her two petticoats under a freshly cleaned gown. The second petticoat seemed unnecessary after such a string of long days.

The two lady-elves met outside the heavy door of Marilla's. Haven wore a simple, black, linen tunic with black embroidery, her own clean hair in its wild red glory, puffed around her face. As soon as they entered, Ella heard the house band playing a ballad.

By ten o'clock she had lost track of the number of shots Haven had ordered for her. She thanked the Spirits that alcohol did not affect elves the same way it affected humans. Still, the alcohol was helpful. The last tendrils of her worry over Hunter University unwound themselves from her heart and she simply began to enjoy the night.

Cheers rose up from the Glima pit. Ella glanced over the balcony railing and into the pit. The next two fighters were battling for the winning spot in the evening's tournament. It wasn't a championship, because it was only a weekday. Therefore, there weren't any well-known fighters left. The honorable fighters graciously bowed out before the final round.

Haven took a spot next to Ella on the balcony.

"Ew, they are so sweaty," Haven said. Ella watched silently, flexing and moving her muscles along with the fighters as though she herself were fighting in the ring.

The winner had good moves: fast hands. As she felt the fighter's movements in her own muscles, her shoulder brushed Haven's, but it went unnoticed. At one point the taller fighter lifted his arm over his opponent's head. Ella's hand started to shoot up, too, as though it had a mind of its own. Haven gave her a weird look, and she pretended to be fixing one of her curls.

Neiman sounded the ring bell which brought Ella out of her trance. She glanced over next to the Glima pit where Oliver had emerged from the wash room. He must have fought in the earlier rounds of Glima and bowed out. When their eyes met, an unidentifiable emotion shadowed his face before his normal scowl returned.

The final bell rang. The night's tournament was over.

Ella left the balcony and joined Haven at her high table. Haven spotted Oliver too, and wrapped him in a sisterly hug. Although he bowed out of the weeknight's final, he had won all of his rounds until doing so. Haven was not the only lady-elf to seek out Oliver. Many pushed their way forward to try flirting with him.

As Ella sat at their table, she had a curious thought. Had Oliver Agnarsson, famous Hunter, bane of the Shadow ever not been a famous Hunter and Glima master? They had learned the basics of Glima together when they were wee. Oliver had sneaked into Marilla's before any of them were old enough and brought back new moves to teach them. A smile teased the corners of her lips as she thought of the serious boy sparring with her and Emil by the river. She did not remember who won those fights, but she did remember giggling a lot. His gaze landed on her over the sea of fawning ladies and she choked on her sip of ale.

Ella looked away and hoped he wouldn't notice that she had been staring. She ran her fingers across Megs' fern flower necklace and felt the sudden need to adjust the bodice of her dress.

"Ella," he said chidingly.

"Oliver." She tried to match his condescending tone.

"Getting a head start on hand to hand training?"

"Definitely." She had forgotten about that. Sometime in the not-so-distant future, all of the Hunter recruits would undergo hand to hand combat training. It was mostly Glima. While the majority of elves participated in Glima as their favorite sport, Hunters mastered it to use in combat.

A drum beat began to rattle Marilla's. The sconces dimmed. Seven drummers began the music for their last musical set of the evening. Soon the other musicians joined in, and the rhythmic tune wafted up to the balcony. Ella loved the dance numbers that were heavy on drums. They seemed to pulse through her very veins. She looked around as dozens of elves entered the dance floor.

When her gaze returned to Oliver, she noticed that his hand was held out to her. He couldn't not invite her to dance, it would have been poor manners. Surely, he would switch partners as soon as they reached their first spin. It was equally poor manners for her to refuse, so she dried her sweaty palms on her dress and took his hand.

To Ella's surprise, Oliver could dance. He seemed to use every muscle to create a strong frame and led her around the dance floor with a secure hand. He sent her spinning and turning whenever he pleased so that Ella's platinum curls flew everywhere. And he didn't switch partners. Ella's feet began to feel light, as though she were a dandelion seed floating on a spring breeze. The smile on her face felt strange after months of stress and heartache. She wasn't thinking about Emil or Hunter training or missing Megs. She wasn't thinking about anything except the dance and the music.

The musicians began another musical treat — a group dance. Oliver and Ella, rather than choosing new partners, lined up across from each other. Every elf in Alveland knew the steps to these folk dances. They ought to since they'd been doing them since their earliest ability to walk.

When the musicians began a ballad, Ella's cheeks flushed. "I need water," she said. She turned to leave, except there it was again, Oliver's hand being offered to her. Ella supposed water could wait. It was unlikely that she would perish from dehydration before the end of this song. Oliver pulled her gently into place, up against him. His face held its usual, brooding expression. If possible, it was even more serious than normal. She felt an unfamiliar energy rolling off him — maybe even something happy, but she couldn't place it. He hadn't let the color out.

Ella placed one hand on Oliver's shoulder, and one in his hand. Many elves had left the dance floor, so she felt as though she and Oliver were suddenly on display. Haven raised an eyebrow at Ella. Her cheeks grew hot again.

When the fourth song began, Ella didn't know what to do. She had danced three dances in a row with Oliver. Three with Oliver. Even though they had just finished a slow dance, they were both breathing heavily. Oliver's gaze ran over her face and lingered on her mouth. Warm tingles spread through her body where his hands were still clutching her.

It almost looked like he wanted to kiss her.

Her stomach did a somersault. She didn't want Oliver to kiss her. Maybe she did a little bit. Panic flourished in her chest. "I better go check on our table. I mean I better check on Haven. I mean she's at our table." Ella fled.

"What is wrong with you?" Haven scowled at her. "Oliver looked like he was about to kiss you."

"I know. Hence why I came over here."

"What is wrong with you?" Haven asked a second time.

Ella shrugged. Where to begin.

"What is your whole thing with Oliver? Because you were wee together? Because he pulled your pigtails and teased you back then? Look at him now, Ells. He's not wee and neither are you." Ella glanced over her shoulder towards the six-foot wall of solid muscle. He was by the door tying his elvish cloak around his broad shoulders. His dark hair flopped into his face, blocking his expression.

Two lady-elves hovered close to him, but he didn't pay them mind. Ella didn't want him to go. She had wanted to kiss him, and that scared her. She couldn't kiss Oliver. And he couldn't kiss her. Ella had been in a relationship with Oliver's best friend for her whole life. She pushed her way through the crowd, but by the time she reached the front door he had left.

Chapter 17

Bunked

Sunday, October 9, 1899

Oliver breathed in the salty air. In the pitch of morning darkness, he lurked behind one of the boulders near the ship. It was a Hunter ship — The Aerilee — a mammoth, doorless vessel, that had carried them on many adventures, most in the name of chasing the Shadow. All of their chasing efforts had been in vain so far. Whether or not they were able to catch the Shadow, he couldn't wait for the Aerilee to convey him away to the sea center, where he could properly breathe.

Oliver was slowly making a disaster of his life. He had one secret, which he had successfully suppressed for twenty-seven years. A secret that had caused him unending misery, yet also spurred him onto fame and goodness. He had come dangerously close to blowing the whole thing because of a little pub dance. At least he was still a Hunter, and a damn good Glima fighter. For some odd reason, his father was trying to taint his Hunting euphoria by assigning him to the wrong team. However, he would shortly rectify that, just as soon as he was on that boat.

Oliver watched the crew readying the boat. Many were hired hands from the Palace Province. The Hunter crew could keep a boat afloat on their own, but it was always a relief for them to have a sailing crew. Especially when they came to a difficult battle and ended up with Hunters who needed rest and healing on a return voyage. The Hunters arrived in the darkness, each with their Hunterpack. One by one, they boarded the boat along the gangway. Everyone boarded except Celvin, their leader. That's not how Oliver would run things if he were leading the attack team, but it seemed good enough for Celvin. Oliver shouldered his Hunterpack and climbed aboard. Several of the Hunters nodded to him, as did the crew. They could see that he was where he belonged.

Oliver quickly unpacked his few belongings into one of the bunks below deck and left Onyx on his bed. Then he returned to the deck. This trip would surely help him get his head back on straight. On Friday he had almost tried to kiss Ella. Ella. Emil's former fiancée. Ella. Something had come over him. Whether it was exhaustion from fighting or the music or the recent encounter with the Shadow, he had completely lost his mind over a pair of sky-blue eyes and blonde curls. The cut of her dress bodice hadn't helped matters, and he had almost kissed her.

With a bit of elvish luck, he would leave on this trip, defeat the Shadow and retire somewhere in the mountains, never to be seen by Ella again. But even if they didn't defeat the Shadow, it would be years before he returned to the Palace Province. This trip had definitely arrived at a good time.

Oliver hadn't even wanted to go back to Marilla's for the Glima tournament on Saturday, but he had. Surely someone would have come looking for him if he didn't register as the reigning belt-holder. Regardless of his hesitation, he had shown up for the tournament and won the belt a second week in a row. And even better, had not seen Ella.

He also had not seen Haven, who had given him an earful on Saturday morning at their Hunter Summit. She had obviously seen his odd behavior on the dance floor. As Ella's room-mate, she was looking out for Ella's well-being. Good thing he was a famous Hunter who could look out for himself and everyone else in Alveland for that matter. It would have been a most disastrous choice to kiss Ella. He was surprised at how little control he seemed to have had over himself at that moment in Marilla's.

Oliver leaned over the port-side rail and took in the sight of the little harbor waves crashing against the side of the ship in the light of early dawn. He could feel the anticipation of adventure rippling through his veins. The boat would launch at sunrise. Where was Celvin? He was going to miss the launch. Oh well, then Oliver would just have to lead the attack team mission — like usual. That didn't sound so bad.

Lindy leaned against the port-side rail next to Oliver.

"Where's Celvin?" Oliver asked.

"Here," Celvin said. "With the Commander."

If possible, it went worse than Oliver could have expected. First, the Commander called off the attack team mission. The energy from the crew and the Hunters was off at the arrival of Commander Agnarsson. He declared that the mission was cursed before the ship left the harbor, so everyone deboarded and the sailing crew rolled up the sails. Then, the Commander marched Oliver off the ship, like a disobedient wee being sent to his room. They walked in silence all the way back to the Commander's quarters at the palace, ripples of black angry energy swirling between them.

Once inside, Commander Agnarsson spoke first, but Oliver cut him off.

"I should have been on that mission."

"You should have obeyed orders."

"Your orders were wrong."

"You were needed on the retrieval team."

"No one is needed on the retrieval team. The retrieval team is a joke — no one is ever found."

"Well now you're not on any team."

"I'm on the attack team,"

"You're bunked."

Oliver's jaw dropped open. No. He couldn't be bunked. In an act of desperation, he tried to be respectful to his father. "I… I shouldn't have shouted. And I shouldn't have disobeyed orders."

"It's too late. You'll be assigned here, training new Hunters. Indefinitely."

"Another great way to be rid of me," Oliver said.

"You're a hundred sixteen years old. You're responsible for yourself."

He always had been. In fact, it was better this way. If he hadn't been on his own as a kid, he wouldn't have grown up tough. And if he hadn't grown up tough, he wouldn't be the successful Hunter he was now. He didn't need his pa when he was wee, and he sure as hell didn't need him now.

Chapter 18

Glima Training

Saturday, October 16, 1899

Ella pulled on the stretchy cotton pants that hung in the back of her closet, intended to be worn under her tunics. At least they were clean, now that she was a successful launderer of clothing. She pulled on a short shirt, intended to be worn above her belted skirts. She heard from Haven that the attack team had considered embarking upon a mission last week to pursue the Shadow and that Commander Agnarsson had canceled it.

Ella wrapped her hair into a tight knot at the back of her head, which left her neck free and cool. She washed her face and ate a baguette she had made last night at the Holding's. Then she left the Amarind Building and headed to Marilla's.

Not all Hunter training took place at University. Glima training would take place at Marilla's. When she arrived, Ella could hear the voices of the Hunters in the Glima pit. Ella did not know what Hunter Glima training would be like. Sure, she had fought before, but not in public. She remembered liking it as a wee one, but certainly she would not as a grown lady-elf. And not with a bunch of Hunters.

"This is for you, Megs," Ella whispered. She wrapped her hand around the fern flower necklace as she descended the creaky, wooden stairs toward the Glima pit. The closer she got to the dirt floor, the more stench made its way into her nostrils. She smelled sweat and dampness, and was that also mixed with the smell of blood? Her nose wrinkled at the thought.

Ella seated herself amongst the eighteen Hunters-in-training along the front row of tables, closest to the Glima pit. Twenty of the forty-four veteran Hunters were present as well, sitting toward the back of the room. Ella waved to Haven. Ella suspected that Haven loved Glima. Commander Agnarsson entered Marilla's and seated himself next to Oliver who was speaking. Ella could feel the tension between the Commander and Oliver — it was worse than usual.

"Starting immediately, Hunters will teach basics and execute several demonstrations. Following instruction, the trainees will pair off and spar." The voice hit Ella with irritation as awful as a persistent mosquito in the ear. As the reigning belt holder in the province, it only made sense that Oliver would be running the training. But when she heard his voice and saw him standing there in the center of the Glima pit, something began to burn within her. It burned like scotch down the throat. Ella felt inspired. If she had to do Hunter Glima training, then she would bring the fiercest competitor to the Glima pit for each match — the one within herself.

Ella did not pity herself any more. In fact, she began to get excited. Sure, Oliver had saved her and helped her survive her first day as a nanny, but that didn't make up for what he had said on the high rope course — that Megs would never be found. And it didn't make up for their year of hell before he left for the Far Lands. If she had the opportunity to fight Oliver Agnarsson, Spirit of the Ocean, she would seize it, and she would take him down.

The burning feeling engulfed her and she began to have a difficult time paying attention. Bear delivered a mug of ale to her, but she barely noticed. Suddenly, all the noises in Marilla's began swimming together. Everything was Glima.

The pit area opposite the Hunters was packed with a light afternoon crowd of Glima fighters and Glima fans — mostly lad-elves. A few lady-elves who were being courted by fighters were scattered here and there. They stood out like polka dots on a tablecloth because of their long dresses. The championship match wouldn't be for another five hours, at eleven. At first, it would just be one-off matches. The dozen or so winners wouldn't start fighting each other until nine.

Ella stood ringside with the other trainees as Oliver began instruction with the veteran Hunters. She felt Alveland's energy as her feet rocked in motion with whoever was fighting. Each hold, each takedown, each duck and escape she felt surge through her muscles in her own, private phantom match. Her mind started whispering moves to her in advance of the competitors.

Squat, shoulder, duck, tuck, spin, hold, grip, spin, throw.

Cross-step, cross-step, grab, grab down.

Spin, cross, squat, grip, lift throw.

The clock on the wall struck seven p.m., and training began. Ella was called into the pit with the other trainee Hunters and lined up across from a partner, Magnus. He ended up flat on his stomach with his face in the dirt. The Hunters rotated partners. She faced Derrin. She did an under-the-throat takedown, so he went sprawling across the dirt and into the sparring pair next to them. Upon another rotation, Ella faced Barnon. Ella's Barnon takedown landed him on his back.

Ella had forgotten how fun it was to fight. She stretched all her muscles as she waited for her next partner to rotate. A small self-satisfied smile crept onto her face, one she couldn't control. Until she caught sight of Oliver. He cleared his throat and looked away when she saw him. She really hoped she would get to fight him tonight. But how? Would he deign to fight his trainees?

After an hour, the Hunters were dismissed from their instruction. Several left. Some stayed. Neiman, the keeper of the fight schedule, gave the first call for the night's fighters. The tournament was about to begin. Ella felt like she was at a crossroads. No one in Alveland knew that she could fight. She didn't even really know it herself because it had been so long since she'd done it. If she fought, it seemed like the final nail in her Princess coffin. She really would be leaving behind her old self, and needing to discover a new one. Or maybe rediscovering a very old self. Without meaning to, her feet had climbed her over the rope and over to Neiman.

"Did you sign up to fight?" Haven had appeared next to her.

Ella could barely believe it herself.

After teaching his lessons, Oliver slunk into the shadows as far back as he could. He looked out a small window on the basement floor and drummed absent-mindedly on the window frame. How did he get here? He was teaching Glima lessons in the basement of a bar instead of chasing the Shadow. If no Hunters pursue the Shadow, how will anyone ever know if the Wicked Three are really behind it? With the Hunters on this ridiculous furlough, the Shadow will continue to travel the elvish lands, wreaking havoc. He didn't know what his father's problem was, but Oliver knew that he should be leading an attack team after it, right now.

Neiman was far enough away that Oliver couldn't hear the names of the fighters being called to the pit, but chatter surrounding him indicated that a lady-elf had signed up to fight. Oliver had a suspicion that he knew who it was that had signed up. He pushed forward into the crowd where he could see Ella's curly hair knot. The corner of his mouth twitched upward. He and Ella had learned Glima together as wees. They'd sparred by the river. She'd won too many times for him and Emil to ever admit. There was something different about the way Ella fought. She couldn't possibly remember much of it now. After all, she had spent a large portion of her life training for the Princesshood.

Oliver was thankful that it was Saturday. The weekly Glima tournament would be a good way to get out his aggression over his father and the Shadow. And his and Ella's mild disdain and annoyance for each other suited him — it allowed him to keep his secret love for Ella to himself. Elves lived to be about two thousand years old, so, he'd only have to keep it for another one thousand eight hundred eighty-four more years. With a little elvish luck, though, he'd get out of the Palace Province soon which would make his life much easier.

Oliver decided to nourish his body before the tournament. He first went to the washroom and splashed water on his face. It was refreshing after his afternoon of instruction. Next, he went upstairs to the bar. He waited for Bear — for a long time. He finally looked down the bar and saw Bear dreamily flirting with a pretty, young lady-elf. Oliver walked over toward the two of them, but as he approached, an old lad-elf spryly took the nearby stool. He was a famous Hunter. And the Palace Province Glima belt holder. Why was it so difficult for him to order food at a local bar? He just wanted a fish mix sandwich and an ale.

Oliver sat back down at the far end of the bar and hoped that Bear would notice his scowl soon.

Ella glanced across the pit at her opponent. He was younger than she. He spoke to Neiman and made a gesture toward Ella. Neiman shrugged and urged him to continue. The young lad-elf had obviously never fought a lady-elf before.

It was the first of five Glima rounds that evening. Though she wished it hadn't been, her name was called first. Ella climbed into the pit. A few elves began speaking to each other, glancing her way. She felt like a lost, feral animal. Let them whisper; fighting felt great.

Brittany suggested she return home so she wouldn't make a fool of herself more than she already had. Ella didn't heed Brittany any more. Ella's stomach fluttered with the good kind of excitement as she glanced around Marilla's basement. There were skilled, regular fighters from the Palace Province, and many Hunters signed up to fight. Instead of feeling intimidated, Ella began to feel her thumbs tingling with anticipation. It had been so long since she had done any fighting. It had been so long since she'd done anything. This was a good change.

Ella and her opponent grabbed forearms, the traditional act of sportsmanship which begins a match. Then, Ella twisted her bare feet down in the dirt and drew out earth's energy. It surged through her and she was filled with a thrilling power. Her opponent, Jökull, circled using his cross-steps, as was customary, and Ella did the same. After two complete circles, she figured he would never make a move toward her. So she took two running steps forward, gripped his bicep with one hand, gripped the back of his neck with her other and threw him to the ground. Then she crouched by his hip, shoved his face in the dirt with her arm and backed away for the victory.

Time and sound seemed to stop in Marilla's. Ella's opponent stood up. Dirt crusted to his cheek and his mouth hung open in shock. All the elves on the basement floor were staring at her, but Ella didn't mind. She couldn't wait until her next round of fighting.

Neiman called other fighters to the pit and the crowd returned to its normal buzz. Ella sat next to Haven, watching matches from the shadows of the basement. Unlike her, most did not take down their opponent swiftly. Many were evenly matched and just when it looked like one was about to be the victor, the other would make an effective counter-attack. Once all the fighters had participated in round one, there was a ten-minute recess before the start of round two.

Finally, Neiman walked to the center of the pit. He climbed over the rope and nervously blotted his forehead with a towel. "Bear and Miss Ella."

Bear signed up for some tournaments, but not every weekend. Ella climbed into the pit.

"Ella, my sweet. If you'd like to spend time together, you could have just asked. We don't have to fight."

A small smirk teased one side of Ella's mouth. Leave it to Bear. The two grabbed forearms. Ella cocked her head to one side, suddenly amused by Bear's appearance. Beneath the boyish face and extra pudge was a real, strong lad-elf.

Everyone in the Palace Province used to whisper about Bear. They used to whisper specifically about his parents. Rumor had it that one of them had been a troll and that's why he wasn't as handsome as all of the other lad-elves. They talked like that until his parents were killed. They were identified as Hunters who had died on the job. With them gone, Bear took care of his younger sister for them. No one whispered about him after that. Looking at him now, in the Glima pit, Ella felt like she was seeing him for the first time. Too bad she'd have to take him down anyway.

"You know, Bear. You look kinda handsome without a shirt. You've got a bunch of muscle under there."

Bear smiled. He cross-stepped to begin their circling.

Ella decided to take a different tactic with Bear because of his size. She'd let him come to her and she would stay on top of whatever he did. He squatted and lifted her against him as though they were doing a well-rehearsed dance lift. Up above Bear's head, Ella rolled her eyes. Bear grinned. She looked down at him, calculated her victory and asked him, "Are you ready?"

"Always ready for you, my sweet."

Ella arched backward while kicking her leg under Bear's armpit. She did a perfect backflip, landed in a crouch and side swiped his feet. His arms were under him, so she knew he could make an escape and take her down with him, so she knelt quickly by his side, trapped one arm behind his back, pushed his face into the dirt and backed away the victor.

That priceless, stunned-male expression never seemed to get old.

"His Highness, Prince Emil and Miss Ella," called Neiman.

Emil was a great Glima fighter from the Palace Province who had been belt holder many times. When Neiman called Emil's name Ella's head shot up. She had been so caught up in her annoyance with Oliver and her excitement for Glima that she had almost forgotten about Emil, her former fiancé — the Prince of Alveland who almost married her. Emil had won his match. Watching Emil fight made her think of the grassy knoll by the Fainde River. She, Emil and Oliver used to fight together all the time as wees. The grassy knoll was their favorite spot for sparring. They liked it there, because when they started to sweat, they could jump off the rope swing and cool off in the river.

"Wait you have to fight Emil?" Haven sounded horrified for her. Ella was grateful that Haven was there, next to her, but she also missed Megs.

"Have to?" said Ella. "I get to. It's not often a girl gets to fight her ex." Haven covered a smile with her hand.

Emil was bigger and more muscular than Jökull, but much smaller than Bear. Plus, being engaged to someone your whole life had its advantages. Ella knew that Emil had a scrappy personality and speed which often won him the victory. One of Emil's earlier fights had earned him a huge gash above his eyebrow. As in the beginning of the other matches, she dug her toes into the dirt and reveled in the feeling. It seemed that Alveland was rooting for her. And it surprised her to realize that she was finally rooting for herself.

Emil approached her in the middle of the pit.

"Do you want to talk first?" Emil asked.

"Nope."

Ella was pleased to see the sudden look of self-doubt on Emil's face. What one said to an opponent before a fight was an important part of the game. Who's to say Ella wasn't good at that, too?

They grasped forearms. Ella cross-stepped and began the ceremonial circles. When she was ready, she charged toward him and grasped him and prepared for her favorite throw down move. Unfortunately, as she plunged him toward the ground, he caught her behind the calves with his hand and pulled her feet out from under her. They both ended up in the dirt.

Ella popped up first. She took a moment to revel in the freedom of her stretchy pants and lightweight shirt. She still thought she looked ridiculous in Hunter garb, like an odd little lad-elf. But she didn't care anymore. Petticoats had lost their sensibility.

Being an honorable opponent, Ella waited for Emil to return to his feet before taking him down with finality. She spun with her back to him, placed a hold around his throat and dragged him down. She pinned him to the earth with her hands and one knee and backed away the victor.

Everyone in Marilla's was now watching Glima. With the final and championship fight upon them, many elves were packed onto the staircase, further blocking the lights from the upstairs chandelier. The Glima pit now depended solely on its downstairs sconces for light. People at the balcony bars stood shoulder to shoulder, creating a sea of heads. Ella found a surprising indifference toward the crowd. She didn't really care who was watching, she was grateful to get to fight again.

Neiman called her and Oliver to the pit. She would have to take him down twice to be the victor, and she couldn't wait to do it. This was what she had been waiting for over the past five hours — maybe longer.

"Ells. Are you nuts?" Megs would have asked.

Ella would have answered, "Megsy, don't tell me you have a problem with a shenanigan."

"Nope. Just surprised that my Princessy friend is the one doing the shenanigan."

Megs would have been proud of her.

Ella smiled and ran her finger over the bumps of her fern flower necklace, then tucked it into her linen shirt and out of the way for the fight.

Ella climbed into the pit and watched Oliver saunter forward. His muscles rippled mercilessly across his arms and chest which glowed in the chandelier light. Apparently, the attraction she had felt for Oliver on the dance floor and on the rope course had not disappeared. Who could blame her.

"I don't suppose you want to talk things out before we do this?" Oliver asked.

"You lad-elves are awfully chatty tonight," Ella said.

There it was again. Undetectable but for being close, Ella thought she saw an upward twitch on the corners of Oliver's mouth. It looked positively foreign.

"Fight," said Neiman.

Ella and Oliver grasped forearms. Oliver began the circling with a cross-step. Although he was lean, he towered over her. That meant she would have to avoid a choke hold, or anything that might involve him rolling on top of her. And she obviously couldn't do an over the shoulder takedown since she wouldn't be able to lift him.

She'd have to play it scrappy — like she did in Mannland when she took Oliver down over and over again in the snow. She would win if she beat him two out of three rounds.

Ella took the offensive, first. She lunged toward Oliver who grabbed both of her upper arms.

Damn.

Adrenaline pulsed through her body. She glared into his eyes, and circled her hands in order to break his grasp. It was easily accomplished. Once free, she spiraled her right arm around his, stuck her elbow into the soft flesh above his bicep and executed another perfect slide by, just as she had with Jökull. Oliver caught his balance quicker than Jökull, though.

No matter, she simply used her shoulder to give him an extra shove before sweeping his feet out from under him and backing away the victor.

"Damnit," muttered Oliver under his breath.

Some cheers rose up from the crowd.

Ella felt that little self-satisfied smile tugging at the corners of her own mouth. It felt strange, like a pair of shoes that had grown too small overnight. Neiman called them back for a second fight. Ella and Oliver grasped forearms.

Oliver brushed his dark hair back from his face, but it immediately flopped forward again. Ella chided herself for noticing Oliver's hair. This time he moved first. It was a good move, too. He grasped her behind the neck causing them to circle tightly with their bodies hip to hip.

Ella smelled his oceany scent. In her mind, she heard an ocean wave crash against the shore. If she strained with her elvish ears, she could hear an actual wave crash against the rocks outside Marilla's. She loved the ocean. She dared to look into Oliver's blue eyes. She saw something besides anger and grumpiness. Sadness, maybe?

Ella lowered her gaze to his mouth and for a brief second wondered what it would be like if she hadn't pulled away from his kiss on the dance floor. His gaze dropped to her mouth as well.

Ella heard another phantom wave crash.

Then, with a whoosh in her ears, she realized she was still circling in the Glima pit. She pushed aside her phantom waves and felt the actual waves of muscles on Oliver's arms, giving off heat as she gripped them.

But she had come back to the present too late. Oliver released her for the briefest of moments before squatting down, lifting her over his shoulder and throwing her — with a surprisingly gentle roll — in the dirt. He backed away for the victory.

The crowd cheered. Was it possible that they were cheering for both fighters? It sounded that way.

Ella had dirt on her butt, which she was mad about. Her hair was falling out of its knot, which she was also mad about. And she had swooned at Oliver which made her furious. She stomped over to the corner of the Glima pit to where Haven was standing.

"Uh… Ells?" Haven asked.

"Don't," warned Ella.

"It looked like you were gonna kiss him."

"I said don't."

"My bad. But don't kiss him. Take him down."

"Not a problem."

"Kiss him later, maybe."

Ella rolled her eyes and stomped back out into the pit.

"Fight," said Neiman.

Ella and Oliver grasped forearms.

Ella began circling in the opposite direction Oliver had started them last time. She had always been able to fight from either direction as a wee one. It was something that often tripped up Emil and Oliver when they sparred by the river.

Ella attacked first. She reached for Oliver's neck and arm, but he spun out of her grasp. She yelled and ran after him, instinct taking over. The fight that followed was ugly, and unlike the ones she had done before. They rolled on the ground, grabbed each other's arms and legs, pinched and rolled some more. They paused for a moment, breathing heavily. Ella was on her back and Oliver had both of her wrists pinned to the ground. His torso was sprawled across her own, holding her down with his weight.

Oliver's weight didn't bother her, but her losing posture did.

"Sorry," Oliver whispered in her ear. "I'm going to back away the victor."

Ella looked into his blue eyes once again and saw that other emotion there. Not sadness, exactly, but maybe tenderness. Should she admit defeat? Looking in those eyes, she thought she could be okay with it.

Suddenly, Brittany shouted at her. *Get it together, sister.*

Ella was shocked.

Your legs are free, dummy. Do something about it.

For once, Brittany was on her side. And she was right — her legs were free.

Ella continued to stare at Oliver. She nodded her head. He nodded back, tucked his knees and as he stood up, Ella yelled again. She kicked her legs up so hard her rear end flew off the ground. She took Oliver out at the knees, and at the same time, pulled herself to her feet.

Ella heard lots of gasps from the crowd as she and Oliver faced off again. Ella was relieved to see that he looked, yet again, like his grumpy self.

Oliver advanced and took her in a choke hold. She almost felt like he was hugging her from behind, except she was trapped. Fortunately, she had shifted her weight off to the side before the tie up, so Oliver did not have total control.

He thought he did. She could tell by the way his breathing had relaxed. And then she did that wonderful thing she loved to do so much. That thing that had gotten her victory over so many of her childhood Glima fights. She played out her own victory in her head.

Elbow pop, cross-step, back step, throat hold, drag down, knee lock and back away for the victory.

"Elbow pop, cross-step, back step, throat hold, drag down, knee lock and back away for the victory," she said.

"What?" Oliver asked.

"I'm not repeating myself. I'll show you instead."

And she did.

She executed the steps as she described, and ended the match with Oliver's face in the dirt, her knee in his lower back, her arm across his face and then she stood for the victory.

"Vegari!" yelled Neiman. He brought over Oliver's belt and gave it to her. She took the belt and turned it over in her hands. What the hell was she supposed to do with this? She couldn't help but burst out with laughter as she held it over her head toward the cheering Marilla's crowd.

Chapter 19

At the Keeper's

Sunday, October 17, 1899

Oliver was annoyed to find that he had awoken before first light. And as much as he tossed and turned, he couldn't get back to sleep. He lit a single sconce so he could dress in the solitude of his temporary hunter dwelling in town. Onyx rubbed in between his ankles, nearly tripping him. He wanted his breakfast. Oliver stumbled to the cold box and extracted a filet of fish which he left on the floor for him.

There was something in his ocean Spirit that longed to see the sunrise over the ocean. So Oliver decided to go there. But first, he sleepily shuffled his way to Jandotter's and bought breakfast. He had allowed Onyx to tag along since he didn't have any official Hunter duties today. Onyx nuzzled his hand hoping for a second breakfast which Oliver obliged.

Oliver was less than happy about, well, everything. He was less than happy that he was bunked from the Hunters. He was less than happy that the Shadow was roaming free. He was less than happy that he was living in the same province as his father. He was less than happy that he was teaching Hunters. And he was less than happy that he had lost the Glima belt… to Ella.

After breakfast, he stomped away toward the ocean cliffs. Unfortunately, when first light did arrive, all Oliver could see was clouds overhead, and no sunrise over the sea. Oliver turned toward the mountains. He wasn't looking for anything in particular, but he found something anyway. As the gloomy dawn rose like a mirage out of the sea, he caught sight of the Keeper working his gardens. Of course he would be up early. Sometimes Oliver used to wonder if the Keeper ever slept. Did he sleep?

Oliver tried to circumnavigate the Keeper's property in order to avoid any early morning conversations, but his footsteps were too loud on the gravel footpath, and he was discovered.

"Best morning, young Oliver." The Keeper's voice came from behind the Bendleflower bush he was trimming.

"Best morning." Oliver paused outside the Keeper's gnarled fence. He hoped the Keeper couldn't hear the sound of disappointment in his voice.

"All finding you well this day?"

Oliver scoffed in response. Nothing had been going well, lately. He stretched a sore muscle in his arm, still nagging him from last night's Glima matches.

"Your father is well?"

Oliver nodded, clenching his jaw.

"You don't have much to say of him now, but you did when you were younger."

Oliver shuffled his elvish boots in the gravel.

"You often came to my door as a wee. I let you hide from your nannies so you could attend the noon fights at Marilla's. Sometimes you would come in and sit on the stool in my kitchen. And did wee Oliver ask for lunch?"

He hadn't.

"But I fed you anyway. We both know you needed your father to dry your eyes, but I was happy to do it."

Oliver clenched his jaw. The Keeper peered at him above the bush. "But you don't need him to dry your eyes now, right General? You can do that yourself. Or maybe even have a lovely lady-elf to do it for you. Maybe even a lady-elf who would fight for you."

How was it that the Keeper knew everything? How could he possibly know about his fight against Ella? Let alone his love for Ella.

"I thought we were talking about my father." Oliver's voice rang with bitterness.

"We were. But we can talk about more than one person, if you'd like."

"I wouldn't like."

"Hm." The Keeper clipped quietly at his bush.

Oliver just wanted to get inside the Shadow. He didn't want to let go of the grudge he held against his father and he didn't want to admit that he loved Ella. Those energy-riling emotive exercises served no purpose.

The Keeper began humming 'Queribeth'. It was the elvish folk song his mother used to sing to him. If there were three people Oliver could do without discussing, it would be Ella, his father and his mother. Yet here he sat on a wooden fence post in the Keeper's yard, allowing it to happen.

"What did your father tell you before he made you General?" The Keeper motioned with his head to follow him inside. Oliver didn't want to go, but he knew better than to defy the Keeper. His parents had taught him as much.

"That he loved me and was proud of the lad-elf I had become."

"Hm," the Keeper said. "It sounds like he respects you for who you are, and loves and accepts you."

"But he wasn't there when I—" Oliver didn't want to finish that sentence. He couldn't respect himself if he did.

"Isn't he with you every day now?"

Oliver looked at the mug of tea the Keeper had placed in his hands.

"What did your mother tell you before she died?"

Oliver cleared his throat.

"I bet she told you that she loved you. And that she wished she didn't need to give her life for Alveland, and that she wished she could see you finish growing up."

Oliver remembered the day, too well. He had known something was wrong as the other Hunters deboarded the ship. Oliver could sense the death and blue sadness energy drifting over the taffrails. Commander Agnarsson had carried his mother off the ship down the dock. He carried her through town as though she weighed nothing and laid her on the bed in their town home. His mother lay still in her bed, pale and frail — unlike she had ever looked her whole life.

The Healer stayed with them for a week. He used energy, herbs and mixes, but her wounds from the Shadow had been fatal. The Healer finally called to the Commander who agreed that there was nothing to be done for his wife's wounds. The Healer offered to give her a Mix which would give her strength enough for her final journey to the mountains.

Before she took the journey, she did call Oliver to herself. She told him that she loved him and that she wished she could see him finish growing up. She placed three fingers upon his forehead and told him that she would see him again.

"What did you tell her?"

"Nothing."

"She knew, though, that you loved her. And that you still needed her."

"I cried."

"I remember."

"But you still have a living parent. You both share a deep passion for Hunting."

Oliver drank the last of his tea.

"And for the secret you carry in your chest. You may want to unburden yourself with it. She doesn't know you like your mother did. She can't help you with it if you never tell her. And to point it out, she isn't engaged to be married anymore."

Oliver spun around and glared at the Keeper. The Keeper smiled his wrinkly, closed-lipped smile. "I'll be fine as long as I can get out of the Palace Province, soon."

"You don't enjoy spending time with her, then?"

Oliver stroked Onyx from head to tail, smoothing his fur. Onyx began to purr. It wasn't that he didn't enjoy spending time with Ella. Quite the contrary. But she was untouchable. She was the Prince's former fiancée. She had been his childhood playmate. She was the daughter of two Advisors. Not to mention an altogether infuriating lady-elf. She was, possibly, even more infuriating than a buzz fly in August — and he was allergic to them.

Oliver would admit that he had been taking lots of lass-elf company in order to distract himself from Ella, and he needed to stop doing that. It wasn't good for his Spirit.

"You have been keeping Miss Ella at a distance your whole life, lad, so that you could be a Hunter. Or maybe you've been a Hunter in order to keep Miss Ella at a distance. But you've been a Hunter all this time, and you've loved Ella the whole time, too. Wouldn't it be less of an effort on your part if you just admitted it to her?"

"Ella was engaged to the Prince of Alveland. Her parents are both Advisors. They'll arrange her marriage for her, probably with another Advisor family."

"Time to meet the King." The Keeper stood up from his chair abruptly and leaned on his walking stick. "There was lightning in his orb room yesterday. You know what that means."

Oliver knew.

"The Keeper needs to be around for a prophecy to take place." The old elf lay down his own teacup and left out the front door, leaving it wide open. He wandered down the road in the direction of the Fainde River and the castle, clicking his walking stick as he went.

Oliver closed the door to the Keeper's dwelling as he left. His nose began to tingle and his hands felt funny — happy and refreshed. The Keeper must have slipped a Mix into his tea. What kind of Mix, he didn't know, but with the Keeper, he knew it was for his own betterment. Oliver followed the Keeper at a distance, but stopped at the Fainde River instead of following him all the way to the palace. Still carrying the feeling of refreshment, Oliver climbed up the path he had repaired the day the Shadow had come to town. It had regrown, now, with grass and a footpath. He ascended the grassy knoll and stood beneath the geometric oak tree perched on top. His fingers twiddled the knot on the bottom of the rope swing. He hadn't jumped — not ever. Not before and certainly not after Ella's accident. Surely it was safe, he had tied the knot himself.

Oliver tugged on the rope. He leaned back and counted down, three... two... one, and leaped. Oliver sailed forward. The breeze ruffled his hair as he sailed out of the shade of the tree and into the sun. He let out a childish whoop as he let go and plunged into the river. When he emerged above the water, he couldn't stop a large, strange smile from spreading across his face. He was surprised to see orange joy energy rippling from him.

He had let go of the rope. Could he let go of his issues with his father and Ella the same way? Time would tell, but it may just be right to try. His mother would have wanted him to, that's for sure. He didn't remember a lot about his mother, but he remembered her being surrounded often by orange energy.

With the Spirits as his witness, Oliver was going to change some things. First, he would stop avoiding Ella. And second, he would stop warring with his father. Maybe he would go visit his father — now. And as far as the Shadow, the Shadow took his mother from him. Surely it would be back, and he could take something back for himself. He was finished trying to control the Shadow; it never did any good. Trying to control the Shadow was like trying to control an ocean wave. He just had to wait for it.

Oliver wandered toward the University. It was due north from the Keeper's. On his way, he saw a man with a familiar gait. A Commanding Gait.

"Son." The Commander recognized his footsteps before Oliver could announce his presence.

The two elves walked in silence for a while.

"The Shadow is on the move," the Commander said. "I'm about to meet the attack team. I'll be listening to their reports. It's headed back this way."

"From where?"

"Far North Snolandic Sea."

It could take months for it to reach them, again. Especially if the Shadow was simply three wicked elves traveling by ship, like the Hunters thought. If it was something else, who knew how long it would take.

"You'll come if you'd like." The Commander smiled, wrinkles creasing the corners of his eyes.

A kiddish excitement rose in Oliver's chest. "Really?"

The Commander nodded. Oliver abandoned his aimless trek to University, and he and Onyx followed the Commander. Was his father thinking of reinstating him in the mission? He certainly wouldn't count on it, but he could hold on to hope.

Part II

Winter

Chapter 20

Winter Solstice

Thursday, December 21, 1899

Ella's fur-lined boots scuffed across the road as she made her way to the Holding's. Three long months had passed since Megs' disappearance. Her tummy ache was three months less painful, yet somehow she missed Megs more. Ella flipped up the fur hood on her elvish winter cloak in order to help keep out the chill. Snowflakes dusted her curls as she reached the front porch. Gunner left the door open for her as he blew by in a huff. What was he always upset about? Ella supposed if she had been at home without her parents she would have been upset, too. Her mother, however, chose to care for Ella and run a shop in town — surely the genesis of Ella's obsession with beautiful elvish clothing. It was only after Ella had grown to be fifty-five years old, or ten in human years, that her mother had joined her father as an Advisor. At that point, Mitsy had become her lady's maid.

"I've left all the ingredients for a stew on the table." Hilda adjusted her husband's winter cloak, pulled up her own hood and the two left out the front door.

"Thank you," Ella called after.

"Wead us!" said Andri. Hee was holding his favorite wee tale upside down.

Kristen, too, offered up a book to Ella as she sucked her thumb.

Ella was only too happy to read to the precious wee Holdings on her lap all afternoon. Although, reading books she had read a dozen times left her mind free to wander. Night was creeping in, and she began to worry about Gunnar. She needed to find a solution to her constant battle with the Holding's oldest child. Otherwise, the energy it took to survive an afternoon at the Holding's would outweigh the currency she received in return. Gunnar hadn't even worn a cloak as he ran out into the snow. Wind whipped against the side of the house. All she could do was hope he came home soon.

"Looka me Solstice dwess!" Kristin had suddenly remembered that she needed to show Ella her newest dress. It was midnight blue and covered in crescent moons and stars.

Ella gasped in exaggerated amazement and crouched down to Kristin's height. "A Solstice dress? Look at how beautiful it is!" Ella smiled and held the dress up to Kristin's shoulders.

"Ma made it fo' me. And she made Andwi a matching vest."

"You have a great ma. My ma used to make clothes for me, sometimes, too." Ella hung the dress back in Kristin's closet for her. The distraction had given her mind something to think about other than Gunnar's whereabouts. Tonight's Solstice ceremony would be serene, for sure, but refreshing. It was an important part of every elf's year, to honor Alveland in this way.

After finishing her books with the wees, Ella placed Kristin and Andri in a pile of toys to play while she assembled dinner. Ella was much more confident in her cooking skills now, and was able to prepare a variety of foods. She ran her fingers through her hair and felt proud of that, too. She liked letting it fly free without the normal shellac Mitsy used to put in. She also liked wearing it loosely braided to one side. Sometimes, she even adorned her braids with flowers, which was fulfilling to her flower Spirit.

Ella tasted her stew. It was coming along nicely. The wind whipped against the house again. It came in with the cold as the door swung open and allowed Gunnar to enter. His hands were blue and snow covered his dark hair.

"Gunnar. Are you okay?" Ella asked.

He rolled his eyes and stomped over to the fire, holding his hands above the flames.

Ella left him alone. That's what he obviously wanted. Ella stirred the stew and turned down the burner. Gunnar stalked through the kitchen to retrieve a drink.

"Would you like to set the table?" Ella asked him.

Gunnar let out a sound of disgust before leaving the kitchen.

"Obviously not." Ella wondered if Gunnar would ever learn kindness. And if he didn't, she hoped he wouldn't become like the Wicked Three. She shuddered at the thought. Surely he wouldn't go that far down this road. Without Gunnar's help — or anyone's help — Ella set the table and fed the family and herself with her delectable stew that warmed the kitchen and their bellies.

After dinner, Gunnar retreated to his bedroom. Ella put the wees to bed and returned to clean up the kitchen. As she scrubbed, she thought of what Commander Agnarsson had said at the Glima tournament. He had declared that she had secret Glima skills. Perhaps she wouldn't be a total burden to the Hunters' mission after all. As she thought of the tournament, the corners of her mouth twitched up into a small smile. On that Saturday night in October, Ella had won five rounds of Glima to win the Glima belt. Through the Glima tournament, she had found a place amongst the Hunters.

After only two months in Hunter University, Ella was put in charge of training the new Hunters in Glima, alongside Oliver. And it wasn't even that terrible — something had changed about Oliver. Even though he never smiled, he didn't seem quite so repulsed by everything lately. Or maybe the change had been in her — she certainly respected him more after being thrown together with him for two months. He was incredibly knowledgeable, and was slowly imparting that knowledge to his students. And she found him a perfectly adequate Glima opponent and one she couldn't beat every time.

Training the Hunters in Glima did mean that she had less time to do her University work before going to the Holding's each afternoon. Still, her Alveland currency was abundant, and her satisfaction was great. Ella thought she could hold onto her duties a bit longer.

A large bell tolled, which meant the Winter Solstice was upon Alveland. With only five hours of light during the day, Ella felt the coziness of winter wrapped around her. Physically, she wrapped herself in her wooly elvish indoor wrap. It was white like the snow and had a row of tassels on each end that she liked to fiddle with. Ella sat on her bed holding a mug of tea, watching the sunrise before lunch.

Haven lay on her bed reading the textbook for her Human Relations class. Ella felt her wool wrap moving on its own. She looked behind her and saw ShaSha shoot his tongue out to capture one of the tassels as though it were a cricket. "Not food, ShaSha," Ella said. She laid out some dried fruit on her bed for him, so he would stop attacking her clothing.

Ella grabbed her lantern off her bedside table at eleven-thirty. She and Haven walked to the elves' normal meeting area, in the field next to the palace, just south of the grassy knoll. Some lad-elves stoked a pile of burning embers in the center of the gathering while the province elves gathered, all with a glowing lantern. Ella stood in her normal place in the circle, where she had always met with her parents. As expected, her mother and father soon joined her. She hugged them and got to introduce them to Haven. Ella had worn her elvish cloak and bunched up her woolen wrap all around her neck and head to keep out the unwelcome chill. Elves could stand a great deal of cold. In fact, many enjoyed it. But there came a point in the heart of winter, when every elf felt too cold without overwraps.

When the King arrived, he began the Winter Solstice Chant. Everything they did during the gathering had a reverent purpose. The light burned low, so as not to override winter's deep darkness. Elves could still see each other with their keen elvish vision. The chanting was low and rumbly. A fitting accompaniment to the solemn gathering. The elves chanted a mourning of their past seasons' crops. They mourned the loss of light, but acknowledged the special place the darkness had in their winter lives. The darkness encouraged adequate rest and made the summer days all the more joyous and sweet. They mourned the elves who had taken their final journey to the mountains, acknowledging their peace, but also the hole they left behind in their families.

Ella glanced across the circle and caught sight of Oliver across the embers the other side of the gathering. She wondered how he was mourning his mother this year. Ella remembered that the brave Huntress had given her life for Alveland when Oliver was wee. Oliver's expression never changed. And the only visible emotion was the usual, brooding grumpiness. However, she suspected that in his heart, his emotions ebbed more on the side of sadness than of anger.

Had she really swooned over Oliver? Twice? The first time was at Marilla's, when he almost tried to kiss her. He had, hadn't he? Or maybe she imagined it. And then when she fought him, there was one moment — clearly another moment of insanity — when she didn't hate him. She didn't want to take him down in Glima. She had wanted something else. It was definitely insanity.

The giant elvish chanting circle around the embers dispersed, and lads and ladies began to regather around the heaters which held hot water for brewed tea and cider. Near each heater lay a spread of dried fruit, potatoes and nuts — all bland winter foods that were readily available in the poorest households. Not that any elves were really poor. Any elf living within the realm of Alveland would consider themselves rich indeed. However, some elves simply had more things available to them. And all had dried fruit, potatoes and nuts.

Ella greeted her parents with a solemn winter greeting. She listened as her parents discussed their affairs in the Ruling Council of Advisors. Her mother had recently been invited to join her father on the Council — a perfect thing to fill her currency now that Ella wasn't at home. And it was definitely something to put Maria Marina's strong mind to good use. While she listened and smiled at the tales from the palace, Haven tapped her on the shoulder.

"I just heard about a new prophecy," she whispered in Ella's ear.

Ella's parents exchanged a look.

"You know about it," Ella said to them.

"We have heard of it, yes," they said.

"When is it coming?" Ella asked.

"They almost always arrive near a Solstice." Mr Marina shrugged.

Prophesies, Ella knew, were always either good or bad. She hoped that this one would be a good one, but with the Shadow's recent visit to the province, she doubted it.

The elves gathered around the nearly spent embers one last time. It was almost three in the morning. The King led them in one last chant, and then extinguished his candle. The other elves extinguished their candles as well and began to return to their dwellings.

As they departed from the Solstice gathering, Ella's keen elvish hearing, detected something across the Fainde River Bridge, beyond town and out in the ocean. She decided to investigate. She was, after all, almost a Huntress and had sworn to protect Alveland. The something traveled at walking pace toward the ocean cliffs. Ella sneaked behind Marilla's and peeked around the side of the building to get a good look at what it was.

It was Oliver. Waves of sad, blue energy rolled off him, down the cliffs and out to sea. He was mourning his mother. Ella's heart hurt for him. She charmed a peony blossom nearby and floated it out to sea in honor of Oliver's mother. A wee bit of yellow energy pulsed from Oliver when he saw the flower. Only briefly. Once he sensed Ella's presence, he reigned in all of his energy.

Ella turned toward University to head to bed. On her way out, she heard a particularly violent wave crash against the rocks. She guessed some of the spray had hit the windows of Marilla's. A wild breeze began to tug at her loose curls. The raging sea, the strong wind and the curious rumble of earth's energy beneath her feet told her that there was a storm coming.

Chapter 21

Ivy

Friday, December 22, 1899

It was a thundersnow, a rare oddity in which there came with a blizzard a righteous thunder and lightning storm as well. Ella could feel Megs. She was sure of it. She was as sure of Megs' presence as she was of the night phlox and ivy that grew in the Holding's garden, now nestled beneath a blanket of snow. On her way out of the Holding's, she pulled up her fur-lined hood. She noticed an oddly green plant sticking up out of the garden. It seemed to have climbed upward and on top of the snow. Ella followed the little trail of ivy, and it wove its way out of the garden and away from the town dwellings road. Her sensation of Megs grew. She walked faster. The ivy curled and wound around grasses and plants. It wove out of town and across the main road. Ella gently touched the climbing vine as it curled its way across the rails of the Fainde River Bridge. Where was she? Ella would have screamed it aloud if she thought it would do any good. She just knew that Megs was alive, and that she was near. She followed the vine toward the palace. Ella's heart beat with urgency. She could feel Megs, but where was she? Was she all right?

Around the palace she went until the vine led her to the ivy-covered door of the human realm. There, the ivy wound its way in and out of the other ivy vines. Ella excitedly pulled back the curtain of greenery and yanked open the door to the tunnel.

Ella was full of uncertainty about what to do next. She ran her fingers over her fern flower necklace. She suddenly wanted Oliver with her to lead her through the tunnel, again, like last time. The tunnel looked very dark. The lack of Alveland energy that emanated from Mannland and into the tunnel was depressing. Cautiously, she stepped her foot into the tunnel and quick as a Sprite lit one of the torches along the wall and held it before her as she crept down the dirty tunnel. She paused and searched the ground for the ivy trail. It had not followed her into the tunnel.

Now, Ella questioned her sanity. Had the ivy simply been searching for other ivy? Was Megs' Spirit in the ivy? That didn't make sense — Megs was a fire Spirit. Had she led Ella into Mannland because she was a prisoner in Mannland? Had the magic only worked in Alveland because Mannland was so oppressive?

There were too many unknowns. Half an hour ago she had been nannying at her regular job, in her regular world. Now, she needed to decide if she should press on into Mannland, alone, or return to the dorm building. Ella peeked out the door back into Alveland and eventually yanked it shut behind her as she turned down the tunnel toward Mannland.

———

Without a sense of Megs in the human realm, Ella found herself looking at the front of John Gregor's, the pub she and Oliver had gone to on the night of the Shadow attack. And the same pub in which she had blackmailed Oliver into letting her join the Hunters. It was one of the few places in the human realm that actually held a sense of familiarity to it. A gust of wind pulled the first few flurries into view and sent a chill down her spine. A dark cloud rolled in from the direction of the sea and covered the comforting crescent moon. Ella searched around her, desperate to pull some of earth's energy to herself for comfort. But not enough was there, not in the human realm. Ella curled her toes in her shoes and pulled her cloak tighter around her in order to compensate for feeling exposed and unprotected. She pulled her elvish cloak tightly around her.

She hid her elvish ears with magic and entered the bar. It was too late to hope that Dagur would be there as it was nearly midnight. She was surprised to find that she hoped to see him anyway. She ordered an ale at the bar.

It wasn't long before two men came over to buy her a drink. She had forgotten that elvish beauty was so radiant in the human realm. A third human came over and asked her to dance. She took his hand and followed him through the lit restaurant area and into the darker dance room in hopes that her beauty would not be on such strong display as in the light at the bar. Stepping through the threshold, she almost bumped into someone tall and blonde who smelled like vodka and cinnamon.

"Dae." Relief swept over Ella.

"May I cut in?" Dagur asked her dance partner.

Although annoyed at losing Ella as his dance partner, he conceded.

Dagur swept her up in an energetic dance that went along with the human folk tune. Like last time, she felt flushed and breathless. She tucked her escaped blonde curls behind her ears as she looked up at Dagur. She tried in vain to hide a smile, but was too damn happy to be successful. Her palms were sweaty, and she couldn't think of anything to actually say to him. A thrill rose inside her when she looked into his face. "It's just so good to see you."

"I began to think you forgot all about me," said Dagur.

"No," said Ella. "No, of course not."

Ella and Dagur were nearly inseparable for the last two hours of the night. Dagur enjoyed cigars and drinks at a high bar table as he introduced Ella to his long line of adoring fans from the community.

Ella swirled the last of her drink in the bottom of her glass. Her feelings were conflicted at best. She thought of

Megs. The whole reason Ella had been led to Mannland was in hopes of finding her, but she had failed. She longed to get back to Alveland to see if she could feel Megs again in the ivy. But she also enjoyed being with Dagur. His charm kept her smiling until her cheeks hurt. She barely noticed what was going on around her when he was close by. She often caught herself staring at his dimple.

The only time he left Ella for any length of time was when his friend, Jason, came to talk to him. Jason didn't take off his cloak, but instead brought Dagur with him out the back door for a private conversation. When they came inside, they were speaking in low, urgent whispers. Jason left without saying goodbye, or acknowledging Ella.

"Jason is a powerful man in the community." Dagur tapped off the edge of his cigar in the ashtray at the center of the table. "I'm grateful he minds me."

Ella couldn't think of a response to that.

"What could be more important to a man than his power?" Dagur asked.

A strange question, Ella thought. She had never considered it before. But she thought perhaps there was something more important. Like being back in Alveland, or listening to the sea, or feeling the Spirits of the trees around her in the forest. Lots of things, actually, seemed more important to Ella than power. Still, she could see how her life might have been more comfortable if she got to sit next to Emil on the throne. It would be more comfortable than making her way into the adult world by way of the Holdings, University and Gunnar.

The musicians continued to play for another hour, and Dagur and Ella didn't waste any of it. She wanted to look up at him and see his face, again, but she felt shy. When she finally did look up he was waiting to kiss her. Ella didn't think humans could see colors of elvish energy, but if they could, they would see ripples of orange joy and pulses of maroon desire spilling out of her as she stood in his strong embrace. Oddly, with her lips pressed against Dagur's, she also thought of the time that Oliver had almost kissed her at Marilla's. When the bar closed, Ella was reluctant to leave. She and Dagur slowly tied on their cloaks without urgency.

"I'd like to see you more," Dagur said. He grabbed both of Ella's hands in his own.

Ella felt a little smile pulling at the corners of her mouth, the way feelings were beginning to tug at the corners of her heart.

"I'd like to be worthy of seeing you more," Dagur said. "I think, someday soon, I will be. Maybe I could even be something great. And I hope that you'll agree to a courtship, then."

Ella couldn't keep the smile to herself any more. Dagur was reluctant to let her walk home alone. In fact, the only reason he stopped insisting was because someone else from town asked him for assistance as they left the bar. Ella quickly took the opportunity to take leave of Mannland. Without the distraction of Dagur, she felt the sinking feeling of dreaded disappointment over her failed attempt to find Megs. Nevertheless, she hoped she would see Dagur again, soon.

Saturday, December 23, 1899

Just keep them alive. That's what Hilda had said. That was easy when it came to Andri and Kristin. Harder when it came to Gunnar because any minute of the afternoon she often felt the urge to kill him.

Gunnar ran down the stairs from his room. When he saw Ella, he glared at her and his jaggedly-cut hair shaded his eyes, making him look like a little Daemon.

"Finish your homework?" Ella asked.

"Yeah." Another lie to be sure.

"Can I see it?"

"Do whatever you want."

He paused at the bottom of the stairs and glanced toward the front door. Then he looked back at Ella, daring her to say it. Daring her to say that he couldn't go outside to meet his friends so he could defy her and do it anyway.

Just like all the other times.

Ella had survived the Shadow and had convinced the Hunters' Commander to allow her to attend University and find Megs. She had gotten a job that she wasn't qualified for and had moved out of her house. She had survived a lifetime of smothering parents as well as a break-up with the Prince. So how was it possible that a sixty-seven-year-old was beating her? That would mean he was only twelve in human years. No more. Ella had an idea.

It was a zany idea, but zany might be just what she needed to survive Gunnar.

She silently stood, made her way to the front door and began stretching. Gunnar furrowed his brow. Soon, his look of confusion was replaced by a look of determination. He took off running toward the door. Instead of using magic to seal the door like in the past, or letting him defy her, and go anyway, Ella reached low, grabbed his trailing leg and lifted him off his feet. She flipped him onto his belly and pressed his head and back into the floor... backing away for the victory.

She crossed her arms and gave him a deadpan look.

Gunnar scrambled to his feet. He fixed his face with another scowl and ran for the door again. This time, Ella reached under his throat and did a drag down.

Gunner got up again, with anger flushing his cheeks. He tried a different approach this time. He checked his hip against hers, which made it very easy for her to step around behind his foot and push his shoulders, knocking him on his twelve-year-old butt. And for good measure, in case he was unsure of what was going on, she flipped him on his belly again so she could back away for the victory.

Gunnar stood again, slower this time. He had tears in his eyes. It must have been hard on his little ego to have his ass kicked by his nanny. It also must have been hard to have to make sure to be a mean and defiant tween every minute of his waking life. Exhausting.

And Ella realized in this moment, that it was also probably incredibly hard on Gunnar to be without his parents for the majority of his life. He stomped up to her and stared with a wild expression. He seemed unsure of what to do next. She offered her forearms and he grasped them. Before she let go, she spoke the rest of her zany idea.

"You win, you can leave this house whenever you want without restrictions and without curfew. I won't even ask you about your homework. I win, you show me your homework when it's done, ask permission before you leave this house, prepare a snack for your siblings upon arriving home from school and speak to me with the utmost respect for authority. Are the terms clear?"

Gunnar nodded through tears of frustration. Ella released his forearms. Gunnar looked at the door, like he might make a run for it, but thought better of it. Ella began circling first with a cross-step. The boy had to catch up with a stutter step, but soon he matched her footwork.

Like Ella's other matches, this one was swift with the victory in her favor. It would have been dangerous and painful for her to fight full strength against someone as small and novice as Gunnar. So when Gunnar ran at her to attack, she stepped aside and stopped him with her arm against his chest.

He almost fell.

He caught his balance just in time for Ella to squat low, grab him around the belly and toss him over her shoulder. She actually rolled him, more than tossed, so he wouldn't end up with a back ache in the morning. By the time Gunnar tried to use his legs for a side swipe, Ella had already backed away for the victory.

Gunnar sat up. He wrapped his arms around his knees and sat in silent pensiveness. Ella had learned from Megs the value of just being with someone, and not talking. So she sat next to Gunnar and mimicked his body language.

"So… my friend Charles said his dad said that some crazy chick showed up at Marilla's one Saturday and kicked the crap out of everyone in a tournament, including Oliver Agnarsson, Spirit of the Ocean. Was that you?"

"Yes. But don't say 'crap' in front of your brother and sister." Ella indicated Andri and Kristin with her head. She had forgotten how much Gunnar and his friends idolized Oliver.

"So… where did you learn how to fight so well?"

Ella shrugged. "When I was growing up, I played with Oliver and Prince Emil almost every day. When they began learning Glima, I did, too. And it just kinda happened. I didn't have to work at it that much, but I did anyway because I enjoyed it."

"You think it's fun?"

"Yeah."

"But you're a lass-elf ."

Ella shrugged again.

"Lass-elves aren't supposed to wear pants."

"I'm a Huntress now. I get a free pass."

"So… can you teach me so I'm good at Glima, too?"

"I can give you lessons in Glima, but the 'good' comes from inside of a person."

"What do you mean?"

"It doesn't matter how good your moves are, lad. If you don't believe in your guts that you can beat your opponent and see yourself doing it in your mind, you'll lose."

"I don't get it."

"How about this. Andri and Kristin and I are starving. Why don't you go make us a snack, finish your homework and report back to the foyer at five-thirty."

"What's at five-thirty?"

"Your first Glima lesson."

———

Ella breathed in the deepest, richest breath of her life after stepping outside the Holding's house. It was twelve past nine. She crossed the Fainde River Bridge and wove through town until she came to the rocky cliffs, just past Marilla's. For the first time all day, she was able to think.

She smoothed her hand over the coarse ocean boulder on which she sat, let down her hair and let the wind whip it into a frenzy. At the same time, she rested her chin on her knees. She felt peace and joy.

I did it. She smiled out at the sea.

A wave crashed against the rocks in celebration.

———

Sunday, December 24, 1899

Oliver stood outside the Holding's front door.

"Oof,.

"There, now, pull from under the throat. That's it."

"Oof."

Those were definitely strange sounds coming from the other side. But did they warrant a trip inside the house? He wanted to see Ella again, but children always brought chaos. If he went inside, he assumed he and Ella could be civil to one another as they had formed a teaching alliance over the past several months. He talked himself into knocking by reminding himself that he had decided to stop avoiding Ella — even though he was in love with her. Hopefully Ella wouldn't ask him to explain his reasoning.

Ella answered the door. Her hair was in a braid off to the side, but a halo of curls had flown out and framed her face. She had a smudge of dirt across her arm and she was trying to catch her breath. "What are you doing here?" A discouraging question, but one that was accompanied by a smile. Oliver thought that meant maybe she wasn't too disappointed to see him.

Gunnar came running around the door. "Ella's teaching me Glima. She's really good. Did you know that?"

Oliver knew that better than most.

"Everything well?" Oliver asked the boy.

"Very good," Gunnar said. "I can do a choke hold and a drag down. Miss Ella says she is going to teach me to do a throw down, too, but I have to promise not to try it on Andri and Kristin." Then he added, "I totally promise."

Ella hid another smile.

Oliver leaned against the archway in the Holding's foyer and watched Gunnar's Glima lesson. Damn if Ella wasn't the best Glima fighter he'd ever met. And damn if she wasn't just as good at teaching. Ella showed Gunnar a particularly powerful hip check. (One that Oliver was pretty sure she had used on him before.) Oliver's muscles twitched with anticipation — he wanted to try that move the next time he fought.

Gunnar tried the hip check, but Ella, of course, dodged it. Oliver kept reminding himself to look around the Holding's so he wouldn't stare rudely at Ella. When he looked at her, Oliver was transported to a simpler time. He thought of the rope swing and he felt his roots. It seemed as though the Spirit of the gnarled oak and the Spirit of the Fainde River intertwined with his own ocean Spirit and felt peace.

Ella demonstrated a spin move and her shirt slid off one shoulder. Oliver felt the familiar pull of his body to Ella, the way he always did. He would need to go for a walk soon and maybe get a drink.

"I'll be going, then." Oliver tried to back out of the doorway. "I don't want to interrupt your lesson."

"You can stay," Gunnar said.

Oliver looked at Ella.

"Actually, it would be great if you could stay," said Ella. "You can teach Gunnar the over the shoulder takedown. I haven't had to use it much because of my size. If you teach him, then I can attend to our meal."

"Go set another place for dinner," Ella instructed him. Gunnar obeyed immediately.

Oliver looked at Ella with curiosity. "Miss Ella is really good at Glima?"

"I am," said Ella. She was obviously proud of the improvement she had brought about in Gunnar.

"Well, I know that. But I am surprised that Gunnar will say that."

"We have an understanding, now," said Ella.

After Oliver's instruction, Gunnar respectfully asked permission to leave the house.

"May I go meet my friends, Miss Ella?"

"Yes. Be home in an hour. Dinner will be ready, then."

Gunnar threw Vex into the hood of his elvish cloak and ran out the front door.

"Mr Oliver, Mr Oliver! Will you read to us?" Andri bolted into the kitchen with an armload of books.

"Mi-ter O'ver. Wead us!" Kristen toddled in with a book and a blankie.

Oliver's insides melted.

He took the hands of the two littles and led them over to the table where he could show them the pictures while he read. Maybe he was somehow nurturing his childhood self as he read to Ella's charges.

Ella felt embarrassed to be in Oliver's presence — as usual. First of all, she was afraid he would be able to tell that she had kissed Dagur in the human realm on Friday. How he would know that, she didn't know. She didn't like how she felt about the kiss, and she didn't want Oliver to know that she had kissed a human. And in case kissing a human wasn't bad enough, she could always feel embarrassed about the day Oliver rescued her — not the day he rescued her from the Shadow, but the day he rescued her from herself. Ella had never been able to let go of that.

"Oliver?" Ella asked.

Oliver looked up from his reading with Kristin and Andri.

"Never mind," Ella said. How could she bring that up? It had been almost a hundred years. She retreated back to the kitchen and sank low into the memory of that day.

Oliver had warned them. Emil, who had always been fascinated by human things, had brought a rope back from the human realm. When he had returned from Mannland, he tied it to their oak by the Fainde River. It worked like any other rope swing in Alveland. This didn't surprise Oliver, but he said it would wear out quickly. Oliver said not to trust the human things because they were not the same quality as elvish things. Emil dismissed him. They used that rope for years, swinging out over the river and dropping yards below to splash. Oliver refused. He said he would never jump off that rope swing, and he never did.

Ella remembered the day it broke. That morning, she and Oliver had gotten into a fight. Ella didn't remember what it was about, but she remembered the waves of gray energy which formed clouds around the two of them. Emil, used to their bickering, sat against the trunk of a tree.

"Reconcile, already, so we can play again," Emil said. He impatiently threw pebbles into the river while he waited for their fight to fizzle.

That set Oliver off. He had told off Emil for bringing the rope swing from Mannland. He said he was being careless with his blessings from Alveland. He said Emil needed to protect Ella from harm, and a dangerous rope swing could kill her. He asked how Emil could protect Alveland if he couldn't even take care of his betrothed. Then Oliver ran off.

Emil was so angered that he chased him, probably in order to give him a proper telling off, and possibly punch him. Ella resented everything that Oliver had said. She didn't need Emil to protect her. She was a great fighter, and she could protect herself. And in her solitude, she jumped off the rope swing. It was on that particular swing out, on that particular jump, on that particular afternoon after that particular fight, that the human rope broke.

Ella woke up at the Healer's. Oliver and Emil were not there, but her mother and father were. Her head ached, and she couldn't move her neck at all. Though she had been cleaned, the room still smelled of blood from her dirty garments in the corner of the room, yet to be laundered. She was wrapped in linens. It took months for her to heal. And months more to regain movement.

The Spirits only know why Oliver came back later that day, but he had found Ella, injured beyond belief. He lifted her from the rocks and carried her to the Healer. If Oliver hadn't found her, Ella would have died. She wouldn't have been able to take her last journey to the mountains — her parents would have had to bury her in a rare, elvish funeral. In the months after her accident, Oliver left forever, for the Far Lands. It was there that he became a Hunter, the best Hunter in all of Alveland. When Ella could finally walk, Emil led her back to the river. The human-made rope swing had been replaced with an elvish rope. Emil said that Oliver had climbed the tree and tied it himself before he left. Emil and Oliver never reconciled. Ella always thought that perhaps Emil was resentful that Oliver had been the one to replace the rope for Ella. Oliver had left when he had been eighty-nine (sixteen) and she had been seventy-two (thirteen). It was difficult for Ella to believe that he had been gone for twenty-seven years.

Ella had been so entranced in her thoughts of her accident, that she had forgotten where she was. When she realized that she was in the Holding's house with Oliver, a warmth settled by her navel. "Oliver," she said again.

Oliver tipped his head in response. Andri and Kristin ran out of the room to retrieve more reading books.

"Thank you," Ella said.

Oliver furrowed his brow, confused.

"For rescuing me."

Oliver shrugged. "Part of the assignment."

"Not from the Shadow," Ella said. Her mouth felt dry. "Thank you for rescuing me from... before. A hundred years ago. From the rocks on the river." She couldn't believe she'd never spoken those words before now. "Thank you for saving my life."

Oliver ran his fingers through his long dark hair. He approached her. Ella didn't know what to expect his response to be, but he pressed her hand gently, then left the room and Ella continued making dinner.

Chapter 22

Prophecy

Monday, December 25, 1899

Oliver's soft-soled boots still made an echoing sound as he walked through the castle's stone hallways. The interior hallway at the back of the castle was dimly lit by fat candles, tucked away in arched wells along the wall. He knew the castle's winding halls by heart because of how much he had played with Emil when they were young. Though they often preferred outside play, a castle did pose as a wonderful place for a wee one's imagination to grow. He descended the half flight of stairs at the end of the hallway and paused next to the skinny door on the right which held the mysterious lightning orb.

Oliver was surprised to have received a sound message from his father, including him in the taking of the prophecy. While he and his father were on better terms, he hoped that his father included him because of his Hunter merit, and not because of familial duty. He wanted to be a man of merit.

Oliver reminded himself to submit to the will of the Commander before pushing open the door. Things would probably go better that way. Oliver also knew that a Commander and a General in unity would be much more powerful to Alveland than a Commander and General at odds with each other. And after all, his father was probably the greatest Hunter Commander Alveland had ever seen.

Inside the lightning room was even dimmer lighting. A group of elves surrounded the transparent orb watching little zaps of lightning vibrate the glass. They were all understandably mesmerized. Oliver could identify each elf except one in the group. He recognized King Frederick and Queen Sophia, who held hands as they watched the orb. They had invited Emil to participate as well. Mr Marina represented the Royal Council of Advisers. Oliver, Haven and Celvin were all present to represent the Hunters. And finally, the Keeper was there. It made sense for him to be there, as Alveland's grand secretary and keeper of elvish history. He recorded all the prophecies that the King brought forth with the help of the Seer. Oliver felt tension between himself and Celvin and himself and Emil, but for once, he did not feel tension with his father, so that was something.

The Seer must be the person who Oliver didn't recognize. The Seer could not bring forth the prophecy without the King, but it also stands to remain that the King could not bring forth the prophecy without the Seer. Since the dawn of time, Kings and Seers have had to work together in unity to bring forth these messages from

Alveland. Oliver noticed the zaps in the orb coming quicker, and with more power. The hair on the back of his neck prickled with the electrical charge that now filled the room. The lightning began to crack so loudly, that the elves covered their highly sensitive ears.

"It's time," the Seer said. He approached the orb and placed a shaking hand on it. It seemed to be held there by a magnetic force. Fear filled the Seer's eyes, but he closed them. Then he held out his other hand to the King. The King turned his King's ring upside down, so the gemstone pointed inward, then he laid it in the Seer's palm. When he did, a great wind erupted from the orb and sent everyone's hair and cloaks flying behind them. The wind continued to fill the room, but the lightning changed to something else.

It became a vision. Oliver felt like he was watching someone else's dream. First, five little blue lights appeared in the orb. They began to change shape. Three became faces, familiar to all in the room — the faces of the Wicked Three — Ohghee, Klayden and Burvanyek. Their faces rose higher in the orb. One light changed into another face. Oliver wasn't sure how many people would recognize it, but he did. The last light became a line. The line wrapped one end of itself around the bottom face, and the other end of itself around Burvanyek. There was a great tug-of-war, and finally the bottom face went out, the line snapped and disappeared, and the faces of the Wicked Three rose to the very top of the orb.

When all five lights went out, the wind stopped. The Seer gasped and collapsed to the floor, his hand finally free of the orb. The prophecy was over.

The King's valet had entered the room and fanned the pale Seer, while Anya, the palace cook, brought him refreshment. Everyone had moved from the Prophecy Room to the front parlor and into the light. Once he had some color return to his face, the King dismissed the valet and cook, so that it was just the private party in the room.

"Tell us, Seer, what our prophecy means."

"Simply? It means that Ohghee, Burvanyek and Klayden are rising in power."

"What about the fourth light?" asked the King.

"A human."

"Do you know who it is?"

The Seer shook his head and took a drink from his water glass.

"The fifth light was the elvish lifeline. It's now tied to that human. He will bring down the destruction of the elvish race."

"Is there anything to be done?" King Frederick asked.

"I suppose." The Seer looked thoughtful. He scratched his scruffy chin. "If something were to happen to any one of the five lights, then the prophecy wouldn't come forth."

"Are you suggesting we kill the human?" Queen Sophia looked concerned.

The Seer shrugged.

"It's not our way," King Frederick said.

"Neither is it our way to betray our entire race to death and extinction," Commander Agnarsson said.

King Frederick agreed. "Do you know him, Emil?" The King asked his Mannland-loving son.

Emil shook his head. "I've never seen him before. I can ask Karina, but she is not from Reykjavik."

"Perhaps he has been in contact with one of the Wicked Three," said the King.

"Perhaps Burvanyek — the lifeline attached itself to him," the Seer said.

"It seems we must find out who this human is," King Frederick said.

"I know who he is," Oliver said.

All eyes shifted to him.

"He is a human from Mannland. He lives in Reykjavik. His name is Dagur."

"How do you know him?"

"I met him at a pub on the night the Shadow attacked. I hid myself and a royal in Mannland when it attacked the palace."

The Seer stroked his chin, again.

"Have you a connection with him?" Commander Agnarsson asked.

Oliver hesitated.

"What is the connection?"

"I don't personally have a connection with him."

Commander Agnarsson gave him a stern stare.

Oliver rolled his eyes and said. "He is… interested in Miss Ella."

"Can you convince her to meet him again?" asked the Commander.

"Don't place Ella in harm's way," said Oliver.

"She is a Huntress, now," the Commander said. "To be a Huntress is to be in harm's way."

Oliver knew that well.

Commander Agnarsson walked Oliver back to his dwelling. For the first time, Oliver didn't mind.

"I have been watching the Shadow very closely," the Commander said.

Oliver was thrilled to hear that.

"It has moved so far north, it is almost out of detectable range, but it has turned toward the North Mountains. It seems to be returning to the Palace Province by land this time. I'm guessing it will return in five months' time."

"No doubt it is heading to the Palace Province again?"

"I have a strong feeling, yes," said the Commander.

"So the prophecy will be proven true or altered in five months," Oliver mused.

"Aye."

Oliver didn't want the elvish race to cease to exist in five months. He would have to go talk to Ella about a man.

Oliver lingered outside the Holding's for some time before finally convincing himself to knock. He rubbed the scruff on his chin, wracking his brain for another way to get information from Dagur. He wished he could go into Mannland himself, but he knew that Dagur wouldn't remember him. He'd have to bring up Ella, and when he brought up Ella, Dagur would want to see her. Oliver finally mustered the nerve he needed to actually knock, but then he heard several elves in the Holding's backyard, so he walked around instead.

"Best day," Ella greeted Oliver. Oliver watched her platinum curls wind their way over one shoulder and outline the curve of her chest. How could so much beauty and infuriation be inside the same little elf?

Oliver returned the day's greeting.

In the Holding's backyard, trees and bushes created complete shade. Ella and Gunnar were fighting barefoot in the cool grass. Right next to the wooden deck was a little patch of earth where the grass was starting to grow thin from Glima fights. Ella must have found a way to include Kristin and Andri, too, because they were in the makeshift Glima pit as well. Oliver watched as Ella taught Gunnar how to go easy on Kristin and Andri and safely take them down without hurting them — the same way she did for Gunnar.

"Miss Ella, when are you going to let me win a match?" Gunnar asked.

"Never."

"What? Come on. You're way bigger than me and I'll never win."

"First, I'm not way bigger than you. And second, I never let anyone win. Everyone needs to find their inner strength and win in a fair fight."

Gunnar rolled his eyes.

"Let's go." Ella reached out so they could grasp forearms.

Gunnar cross-stepped with her and made the attack. Ella flipped him over her arm and he rolled onto his back, the loser. Gunnar got up slowly and dusted himself off.

"I never win."

"You beat Andri yesterday before bed."

"I never win against you."

"Not many people do," Ella said. "What moves did you pick?"

"Huh?"

"Didn't you pick some moves you wanted to do in our fight so you would win?"

Gunnar shook his head.

"Doesn't everyone do that?"

"Uh, no," said Gunnar.

Oliver had to agree with him — he never fought that way. He picked his moves as he went.

"I pick out the moves I want to use to win," Ella said. "I play them out in my head, feel my muscles performing them and then I just do it."

"And then you just do it." Oliver gave her a deadpan look. He turned to exchange a knowing look with Gunnar.

"It's like that time at Marilla's when I… I mean when we…" Ella stammered.

"When you beat me?" Oliver finished.

Ella blushed. "Well when you had me in a hold and I told you all the moves I was going to do to beat you and then I just did it."

"I actually remember that now." Oliver scratched his head.

"Let's try it," Ella said.

She matched everyone up, pitting herself against Oliver. Then she talked through a series of moves she would use to takedown Oliver. Even after talking them through it, she was still able to beat him.

"Now you try," Ella said to Oliver.

Oliver and Ella faced off, grasped forearms, and Ella took him down in two moves. Oliver gave her another deadpan look, this time from the ground.

"What?" asked Ella. "Try again."

They grasped forearms again.

"Wait," said Ella. "What moves are you preparing?"

"Squat fake for an over the shoulder takedown, then side swipe with my left foot. I'll flip you over on your belly and back away for the victory."

"Those moves aren't good enough," said Ella. "No wonder you always lose."

Oliver rolled his eyes. "I don't always lose."

"As soon as you squat, I'll pivot off my left foot and your side swipe won't work. As soon as you do, you'll be off balance and it will be quite simple for me to put you on your belly and win. Stand up and I'll show you something better."

Oliver stood and dusted off his linen pants. Andri, Kristin and Gunnar looked on with interest.

"Try your side swipe starting from a standing position. See?"

Ella grabbed Oliver's hips and pulled them against her side. Oliver began to exert great amounts of self-control to keep his energies inside of himself.

"Step on the other side of your opponent's leg," Ella said.

Oliver looked down at Ella's hands which were still on his hips and tried to pay attention to her instruction. "Now, all you have to do is push them a little." Oliver fell backward and stutter stepped, desperately trying not to fall. "When they try to catch their balance, that's when you crouch down and do the side swipe." Ella demonstrated and Oliver fell over on his ass …as always.

"Maybe I should just stay here." Oliver sat in the grass.

Ella grinned sheepishly.

"You all pair off again and I'll watch."

When all the elves were tired, and Ella had won more matches than any of them could count, they went inside to rest. The children retreated to their rooms for a game, leaving Ella and Oliver in the kitchen to drink cool water for refreshment after Glima.

"Something amiss?" Ella asked.

"The prophecy came." Oliver pushed his way past Ella and into her tiny dorm.

Ella had heard about the prophecy near the time of the Winter Solstice, but she did not know that it had come already.

"The King wishes me to bring you into confidence. He and the Commander have a role for you to play in its fulfilment."

"Is it a good prophecy?"

Oliver shook his head and watched her face fall.

"The Wicked Three gain power. The lifeline of the elvish race is now tied up with a human. It seems that the Wicked Three are using humans — or at least one human — to gain more power. The King and the Commander seek more information."

"But how can I assist?" Ella's brow furrowed as she tried to figure out how she could have anything to do with the Wicked Three.

"The human is Dagur."

"No," Ella whispered her protest.

"Will you accompany me into Mannland to seek information from him?"

"Dagur? It cannot be Dagur. Everyone in Reykjavik adores him. No."

"Though that may be, the King and Commander wish your help."

"When?" Ella asked.

"Right away."

"He can't possibly be involved," Ella said.

"The Commander thinks he might know where the Missing are."

Dread draped Ella's shoulders. The elves thinking Dagur was the key source of Mannland's evil was preposterous — she had never seen a person more adored by his community, man or elf. Surely a do-gooder like Dagur would not be a significant pawn in the destruction of Alveland. Still, Ella didn't seem to have a choice. She was a Hunteress. A Hunteress on a mission to keep Alveland safe and a side mission to find her best friend. If that warranted a trip to Mannland and a discussion with Dagur, then she would do it. Ella had gone back to the Amarind Building and changed into more feminine clothes that would blend better in Mannland. Now, she and Oliver donned their elvish cloaks against the chill. They made their way through the tunnel, into Mannland and back to John Gregor's Old Pub. They drank and ate together while they waited for Dagur to enter the bar. This time, however, they ate without a brutal silence between them.

"How will you do it?" Oliver asked.

"Do what?"

"Find out if he's working for the Wicked Three."

Ella shrugged.

"You can't just ask him if he's been hanging out with Burvanyek, Klayden and Ohghee. You need a plan."

"I'll improvise. Like in Glima."

Oliver rubbed his eyes, hoping to relieve his stress headache. Oliver figured that he had had this same headache that had been following him around ever since he first ran into Ella in the alley behind Marilla's so many months ago.

Part III

Spring

Chapter 23

A Discovery

Monday, June 5, 1900

"Now!" Commander Agnarsson said.

Ella extended her hands out to the side and submitted to her participation in Total Exertion. Magic and energy flew from her fingers. Lightning extended down her arms. Fire, smoke, energy and wind burst forth from her palms and into the open air of the training field. The other Hunters looked on from the shelter of the trees.

Seconds passed, then minutes. The Commander stood across from Ella at the edge of the University training field with his arms crossed and a frown on his face. It was a familiar frown — it matched Oliver's. When the last few crackles of lightning zapped the air and the last breeze rustled by, Ella let her hands drop. Her knees wobbled beneath her and she dropped to the earth. Her stomach lurched and she prayed she wouldn't vomit. The rest of the Hunters lauded and surrounded her. Someone handed her a handkerchief and lifted her to her feet.

Today was her day. The Commander asked that all the new Hunter recruits participate in Total Exertion by this week. That way, they could analyze everyone's energy capacity and the Exerted could restore their energy before the Shadow arrived.

"Miss Ella, Alveland has gifted you the magic of trauma," the Commander said. After months of Hunter classes, Ella knew what that meant. When an elf undergoes trauma, Alveland gifts that elf an extra dose of magic and energy to sustain them. Whether it was from her escape from the Shadow, her broken engagement, her kidnapped friend, or her childhood fall, she did not know, but she did have the extra magic. Ella's magic floated around the Hunters' heads for several minutes. Sparks of light, scents of flowers and bubbles of song swirled in the air, along with a pale pink hue.

"Get her some rest," the Commander said. "We still need to get her back to Mannland."

The person who had lifted her to her feet steered her toward the Amarind Building. It wasn't until they had steered away from the crowd of Hunters that Ella noticed that the elf was Oliver. He led her to the University buildings and hired a cart to drive them into town. Ella fell asleep on the short drive.

She dreamed restless dreams of the Shadow and the portal and Mannland. All the times she had to go into Mannland recently had her on edge. She was on edge because she was a Hunter spy, spying on a friend. When she opened her eyes, she found herself leaning against a strong shoulder which had the comforting smell of the sea.

Ella was surprised to see that Oliver had led them to Megs' shop — her Mix Emporium. They were, of course, able to let themselves in, as none of the buildings in Alveland were ever locked. Oliver lifted the wooden gate which separated the main room from the back counter. He grabbed three jars from the crowded shelves and lay them on the counter. He began skillfully crushing herbs and soaking them in different liquids.

"How do you know about making Mixes?" Ella asked. She was surprised to hear her raspy voice, a common side effect of Total Exertion.

"It's part of training in the Far Lands. Most Hunters pick up how to make healing Mixes on the job as well." He shrugged. "We just need them."

As his back was turned, Ella noticed his broad shoulders and tapered waist beneath his lad-elf shirt. And of course, she noticed his sculpted muscles under the ties of his shirt when he turned back around. Ella knew Oliver was handsome, but she had never really noticed how handsome.

Oliver placed his completed Mix in front of Ella in a glass chalice. It didn't smoke like the one Megs had made her, but it sizzled.

"I'm not sure I can get that down right now," Ella said.

Oliver leaned on the counter and frowned his brooding frown.

"You've frowned at me before. I'm not scared of it. And I'm not drinking a Mix right now."

Oliver turned around once more. Ella thought he might use some sort of force to make her drink the Mix. When he turned back, however, he dropped a calendula blossom into her chalice. It sank fluidly to the bottom and bloomed. Oliver had softened the drink to her Spirit by adding a blossom. Ella's stomach did a flip flop.

"Drink it. That's an order from your commanding officer," said Oliver.

When Ella looked from her drink to Oliver, he raised his right eyebrow, daring her to defy him. Ella rolled her eyes, but sipped. Immediately it felt as though a fog had lifted off her mind. The dimly lit emporium seemed lighter and Ella could enjoy the sensations she felt while seated in her friend's shop. It was ripe with the essence of Megs. She had to be alive.

"I can feel her," Ella said. She took another sip. She felt a bit of Alveland's energy return to her body.

"She's probably alive, then," Oliver said.

Ella was comforted by his comment. It was much better than his comment months ago about never finding the Missing. Ella tried to charm the blossom in her drink to bring it to the surface. It floated upward, but then stopped. A painful zap escaped Ella's index finger and she yelped.

"Ouch!"

"Don't," Oliver said. "Don't use your magic. When I did my TE it took a full week for me to recover — just like every other elf."

"If I use it, will it take longer?"

Oliver shrugged. "Maybe. It also hurts."

Ella could see that, now. She blew across her electrified fingertip and rubbed it, hoping to soothe the pain. Oliver opened the cold box and retrieved a brick of ice. He wrapped it in a towel and pressed it up against Ella's hand. The cool temperature helped.

"Thank you," Ella said. She realized that Oliver was holding her hands and her cheeks flushed. She wanted to pull away in case her maroon energy began to flow, but she also felt safe being close to him. She coached herself in self-control instead.

After the ice, Oliver held her cold fingers between his palms and transferred some of his energy into her. The relief was both wonderful and immediate. Her finger stopped hurting and she felt some of the TE weakness leave her. She sighed. Oliver's lips moved upward at the corners and he let out a quiet, "Hm, hm."

Oliver had laughed. Ella opened her mouth to tease him but she thought better of it. She thought maybe she would keep the memory of the laugh in her heart and hope by the Spirits that she got to hear it again sometime.

———

Tuesday, June 6, 1900

"His hands were all over you," Oliver said.

"We were just dancing," Ella said.

"Feeling your backside and bosom are not part of the dance steps," Oliver said.

"He did not feel my backside and my bosom," Ella whispered and a flush flew across her face.

Oliver gave her a deadpan look.

He was exaggerating. What had she been thinking, including Oliver in her special team squad? She knew exactly why she did it. After months of working together and a lifetime of history between them, Oliver made her feel safe. But that didn't make him any less impossible to be around. Five months ago, after the December prophecy, Commander Agnarsson had asked Ella to assemble a special teams crew in order to help discover the truth about Dagur. She had chosen Haven and Oliver, and the Commander insisted on coming as well.

Unfortunately, the last five months had been fruitless for Ella's team. If anything, their plans had backfired. Just a week into their work in Mannland, Dagur had asked to court Ella, like a proper human gentleman. He had asked Commander Agnarsson, who posed as Ella's father, while Haven and Oliver posed as her siblings. Now, Dagur thought he and Ella were marching toward a marriage, never suspecting that she was of another race, from another realm, spying on him with several lethal Hunters. Now, Ella's assignment required her to enter the human realm several times a week. Every time, she got a stomach ache.

And yet, she had to keep going back to Mannland in order to prove Dagur's innocence. She enjoyed her time with Dagur, and feared that her heart was starting to love him. If she had been a human, she probably would have already fallen for his charm. It would have been an easier task to spy on Dagur if he wasn't so wonderful. He treated her well. He respected her. He always made her smile, and was adored by the entire city of Reykjavik.

In order to clear Dagur's name, Ella decided that she and her team would need to get inside Dagur's house and search it. Of course, this would be dangerous. If Dagur was, in fact, working with one of the Wicked Three, then any elf who entered would be trespassing and spying and an unwelcome visitor if they were discovered.

Another problem with getting into Dagur's house was that neither Ella nor her team was willing to sacrifice Ella's purity in order to do it. She was not to be forced into marrying Dagur or spending the night with him. They needed to find another way.

Eventually, the future of the elvish race would come down to Dagur. The Hunters knew that because of the December prophecy. Ella and her team were hoping to find some useful information before it ended with a fight-to-the-death between all elves and humans. Ella still didn't believe that Dagur was in cahoots with the Wicked Three, but she had to find out. The Hunters had to know for sure, for the sake of protecting the elvish race. Ella admitted that 'the Hunters' now included her — if Dagur was found guilty, she would do what was needed to bring him to justice.

Ella and Oliver finally ran out of verbal ammunition for each other — about the topic of the dance, anyway. The four elves stared at their hands in silence around the table in the little human bar. How to get into Dagur's house… the question sat there in the center of the table, unspoken, yet screaming at them. They successfully established a relationship with Dagur, but had no incriminating evidence against him.

"Ahhh!" Ella screamed.

"Apologies, love." Dagur had scared Ella out of her trance by placing his hands gently on her shoulders. She felt especially vulnerable after her Total Exertion yesterday.

Oliver rolled his eyes.

"We were just talking about Ollie's birthday brunch on Monday," Ella said. "Want to come?"

Oliver's expression turned lethal. Ella felt the gray anger rolling off him, but she ignored it.

"I'd be honored," said Dagur. "How old will you be, friend?"

"I don't know," Oliver's voice was dull. "Ask Ella."

Ella gave him a lethal look of her own. "Oliver doesn't like to admit that he's getting on in years. He'll be twenty-two, soon."

Ella thought Oliver was going to roll his eyes right off his head.

"When shall I arrive at the celebration?" Dagur asked.

"Er… eleven a.m."

"Perfect. Tell me your address."

"Um…" Ella thought maybe this wasn't such a good idea any more. Her face flushed and her palms were wet with sweat. She desperately looked around the table. Haven's eyes were wide. Her glance landed on Oliver who raised his right eyebrow at her and frowned.

"We're the third house on Brayberry Market," Oliver said, coolly.

"Oh you live by the market. I hear that's a peaceful part of town. I'm not familiar with it."

"That's lucky," Oliver muttered under his breath.

Ella kicked him under the table.

"The hour is late, my dear," Dagur said. He pressed Ella's hand. "I must walk Mrs Pigeon back to her house on my way home. She came without Mr Pigeon this evening, and her joints have not been acting well." Ella rose from the table to embrace her fake, human boyfriend and watched as he left through the front door of John Gregor's.

"Nice work," Oliver said to Ella as she sat down at the table again.

"Thank you. I enjoy improvising."

"Yes, it was a successful improvisation."

Ella knew what was coming.

"Except we aren't going to get into his house, we invited him to ours," Oliver said.

"I know," said Ella.

"Yes," chimed in Haven. "Our imaginary house on Brayberry Market Road."

Ella dropped her face into her hands. Maybe that had not been her best improvisation.

Monday, June 12, 1900

Spring was everything. Mountain streams ran with freshly melted snow and joined the Fainde River. That meant that the rapids ran quickly with a thunderous joy, and she could not wait to get outside to hear them. Ella put the last finishing touches on her hair updo. It was almost as good as Mitsy's. She applied a very red shade of lipstick which matched her fitted dress. With haste, she donned her lightweight elvish cloak and left.

Opening the door to the Amarind Building, she felt like the part of her which had been in hibernation all winter finally broke free. She smiled at the crocuses, peeking up out of the snow patches in the Amarind garden. The flowers were finally here to feed her Spirit. She breathed in deeply and detected in the breeze the scents of daffodils, hyacinth, forsythia and pear blossoms.

The dread of her task momentarily rolled off her shoulders as she walked down from the University, past the palace to the tunnel entrance where Haven, Oliver and the Commander waited for her. Haven was also dressed in feminine clothes.

Naturally, the Marina 'family' came up with house trouble on Oliver's birthday. It wasn't even a good excuse, either. Ella told him that they had a family of brown rats living in their house, and one of the neighbors promised to exterminate them, but they all had to live in town for several days at a hotel. And because Dagur was such a hero, he offered to host Oliver's birthday brunch.

This was bound to be a disaster. Ella led the way up the steps to Dagur's home. As a military man, he was paid well and could afford a beautiful house. The walls, walkway and stairs were all made of gray stone. As she ascended, she noticed an ivy plant, winding its way up the trellis, just to the left of the stairs. One of the purple flowers caught her attention, talking to her flower Spirit, she supposed. It made her feel sad, which was strange. Usually, flowers filled her soul with joy and seemed to sustain her very life. This flower made her think of Megs. Ella thought she could almost hear her voice.

Oliver brushed past her in a huff and banged the brass knocker, which brought Ella out of her trance. Dagur answered with a grin. How could he be an elvish oppressor?

Dagur's house was built in the traditional Icelandic way, with a raised bedroom to the left — raised in order to keep the heat in at night, when temperatures could plummet and winds terrorize a fragile human. He had thoughtfully prepared a feast for Oliver's brunch. He made several types of fish and compotes to eat with toast, along with a sandwich spread. A teapot warmed on the stove and the smell of cloves wafted from the fireplace, where he had hung a spice satchel. Ella's heart squeezed. She wanted to get out of there.

The Commander had invited Celvin to Mannland with them, this day, in order that he could show up at Dagur's door with an emergency, leaving the rest of the team to sift through his house for incriminating evidence.

"Help me in the kitchen with our food spread, love." Dagur grabbed Ella's hand and she followed him. When they arrived in the kitchen, the food was completely prepared on beautiful, matching display racks on a large center island.

"Everything looks done," said Ella.

"I know," said Dagur.

Ella's cheeks grew hot.

Dagur wrapped her in a gentle embrace and touched her long curls. Ella felt like she was on fire. Maroon energy of desire was filling her, but she tried to keep it to herself. Although Dagur wouldn't see it, her elvish cohorts surely would. Dagur backed away ever so slightly — only enough to tilt Ella's chin upward and place a kiss on her lips. Prior to meeting Dagur, Ella had only ever been kissed by Emil. (And almost kissed by Oliver.) And now she was kissing the human she was spying on. None of this seemed right.

It turned out that Celvin's interference wouldn't be necessary, because an honest-to-goodness real, human neighbor knocked on the door, and asked Dagur for help.

It was Sweet Mrs Rosen. Dagur grabbed his cloak and slung it around his shoulders.

"The water is still hot for tea," Dagur said. "I shan't be gone more than half an hour." He kissed Ella's hand, and then left.

Guilt swarmed Ella.

"I don't trust him," said Oliver.

"Nor I," the Commander said.

"He's just a human," Ella said. "We can't read his energy like we can read elves, and that's why we don't trust him." The hair on the back of Ella's neck prickled as doubt crept into her voice.

The search began. Oliver headed straight for Dagur's work desk, in the corner of the main room by the window. Sunlight spilled across Oliver's face, creating sharp shadows across it. He opened the top drawer of the desk and rifled through pens and office supplies with his pointer finger. Haven searched the living room and the mud room at the back of the house. Ella stood rooted to the spot, feeling paralyzed. She didn't want to look, because she didn't want to find anything.

The Commander poured himself a cup of tea in the kitchen and started rummaging in the ice box. He then moved into Dagur's bedroom, opening drawers and closets.

"Nothing in the kitchen or the bedroom."

"Nothing here, either," said Oliver.

Haven also found nothing. Ella threw her cloak around her. "Shall we return to Alveland, then?"

"There must be something," Commander Agnarsson said.

Reluctantly, the elves donned their cloaks and tidied up their mess, preparing to leave.

Oliver closed the top desk drawer. When it latched, Oliver's fingernail clicked against something under the rim of the desk. All of the elves did a double take and rushed to the desk for a closer look. A tiny lever rested just to the right of the drawer. Oliver pulled it and a writing desk shot out from beneath the drawer. But it wasn't an empty piece of wood.

"What are those?" Haven asked.

Oliver picked up several pieces of paper. One paper was definitely a map.

Ella peered fearfully at the papers in Oliver's hands.

"Portals," Oliver said.

"This red circle is right next to our portal," the Commander said.

"It sure as hell is," said Oliver. He looked at the last piece of paper, which was a note.

"*Let me know when you investigate. Here's my best guess at where to look*, signed, *PB*," Oliver read.

Haven gasped and covered her mouth with her hand. "You don't think it's Peter Burvanyek, do you?"

"Of course not," said Ella.

"Who else would be looking for a portal into the elvish realm?" asked Oliver.

"Wouldn't Burvanyek already know where the portals are?" Ella asked.

Oliver shrugged.

"Maybe a human is looking for the Hidden Folk," Ella said. She knew it was only a foolish hope.

"Let's go," said Oliver, tucking the papers into his jacket.

"You can't take them," said Ella.

"Why not?" Oliver asked.

"He'll notice," Ella said.

"I've already noticed." Dagur had already returned. He looked unrecognizable. The angles on his face brought dark shadows across it, and he looked positively menacing. Gone was the neighbor-loving, gentle soul Ella had befriended. This was someone else. Dagur grabbed his shotgun from over the door. Quicker than a Taerry Dragon, Commander Agnarsson and Oliver had him pinned to the floor with his hands behind his back.

Ella had never really enjoyed brunches. She had always preferred fancy dining meals, high tea and balls much better. However, of all the brunches she'd endured as the Princess in training, this brunch had to have been the worst.

Chapter 24

Dungeon

Monday, June 12, 1900

"Don't try to run," Commander Agnarsson said.

Oliver walked beside Dagur across the open fields outside the village. The skies had opened, and rain soaked their clothes as they walked.

"You're taking me to the elvish realm," Dagur said.

Oliver and the Commander didn't deny it.

"You'll kill me, there, anyway. If I run, I may escape."

"You can't escape," said the Commander. Oliver could tell that his father's training had kicked in. He was fully prepared to do whatever was necessary to bring Dagur to justice and keep Alveland safe.

"And you won't be killed unless there is no other option," the Commander said. "It's the elvish way. Elves don't kill for power and riches; the way humans do."

"Some do." Dagur's lips curved into a prickly smile.

Oliver thought of the Shadow and Ohghee, Klayden and Burvanyek. He thought of the note, possibly from

Peter Burvanyek found in Dagur's possession. Dagur knew too much, and Oliver didn't like him.

Oliver was in agreement with his father about Dagur and protecting Aveland, but he resented his assignment to assist in taking Dagur to Aveland. He wished his father had brought Haven as his second, then he could stay with Ella. He couldn't believe the guilt he felt over Ella. He had finally developed a relationship with the lass-elf he had loved for twenty-seven years, and he had been forced to push her into the arms of another lad — and a human lad.

And Ella seemed to have fallen for Dagur, and now they'd discovered that he was an elvish oppressor. What a mess. This was why he had resolved never to get married or have children, because he was a Hunter, and his job required all of him. Oliver could never be attached to anyone. He needed to be willing to lay his life down for Aveland without thought of who he would be leaving behind. Even though Oliver had resolved not to avoid Ella anymore, he also would never tell her that he loved her. This disaster with Dagur would pass, and he would move on with his life — hopefully somewhere far away.

This was really his father's fault, anyway. Why should Oliver feel guilty? Now that he'd made peace with his father, grown up from his childhood resentment and submitted to his father's authority, he had to obey orders. His father just happened to order him to recruit Ella's help to wrangle the Wicked Three. Oliver probably would have done the same thing if he were in charge of the Hunters.

When they'd traveled close to the portal, the Commander nodded to Oliver. Oliver grabbed at the air in front of Dagur, grabbed a hold of his eyesight and put out his vision, causing Dagur to curse. Oliver and the Commander continued to lead him to the portal and eventually into the elvish realm.

Once on the other side, Oliver and the Commander enjoyed that first, refreshing breath of Alveland air. Even Dagur inhaled deeply, and some pink color showed on his pale, human cheeks.

The Commander and the General led Dagur around to the front of the palace where, thanks to the Commander's sound message, a thickly staged royal guard escorted Dagur through the palace and down to the dungeon. A guard lit a dim sconce in a wall well and brought Dagur a small portion of food.

"Just kill me," Dagur said. "I won't tell you anything."

Oliver halted and clenched his fists. "We'll see," he said. "Did you know?"

"That you were all elves?"

Oliver nodded.

"Oh, how I wish I had."

Oliver restored his eyesight before leaving. Oliver wanted to say something to him about Ella, but he didn't know what. Part of him wanted to thank him for treating her well. Another part wanted to kill Dagur, like he had requested.

———

Oliver's footsteps echoed as he ascended the stone stairs. It took him several minutes to walk through the guarded hallways to the King's study in the front of the palace. Before he entered, he could hear King Frederick speaking to his father. It also sounded like the Keeper was there, which made sense. King Frederick would want any of the Keeper's wisdom and historical information pertaining to the Wicked Three. Oliver entered the room. He had always liked the King's study. The cherrywood desk was strong and bulky, while the walls of books lent a degree of comfort — comfort that they were surrounded by the knowledge of elves before them. Oliver pulled the papers from Dagur's desk out of his elvish cloak and dropped them on the King's desk.

King Frederick crossed his chest with his fist and bowed.

Oliver returned the respectful gesture, making sure to bow lower than the King.

The Commander, the Keeper, the King and Oliver spread out the papers and studied them. The urgency in the room was palpable. Only the Spirits knew how long they had before the prophecy came to fruition. It was definitely close. Dagur had been brought to Alveland.

The papers were confusing. If necessary, they could give Dagur a truth spell, and he would explain them. However, the less they interacted with Dagur, the better. They didn't want Dagur to feel like he had any power over the elves. One paper simply contained lists of numbers, some of them circled. They didn't seem to form any meaning or pattern. The next paper also had lots of numbers in circles. Was it the number of prisoners? Or the number of elves working for the Wicked Three? Or perhaps it was the number of humans working for the Wicked Three. Oliver didn't know.

Oliver furrowed his brow as they all continued to stare at the papers. He shifted positions as though that might help him decipher what he was looking at. He wanted to find out the meaning behind the papers so he could hurry and get back to Ella. They were supposed to meet up in Alveland later, but if he could leave early, he would return to Mannland and escort her back.

There were several portals between Alveland and Mannland. Oliver knew of the three in the Palace Province, and the three in the Far Lands. Dagur's map correctly identified two of the three in the Palace Province. There were several question marks on the papers near their portal. Had Burvanyek really forgotten where it was? He was an elf after all. Oliver supposed that not all elves paid attention to where the portals were — some elves didn't believe in entering the human realm. The King, after all, discouraged it. Much to the King's disappointment, this never seemed to deter Prince Emil. In fact, it was because of Emil, Oliver had often found himself in the human realm.

The third paper seemed to be a crudely drawn world map, also covered with numbers.

"This number is labeled Reykjavik. Near the city was the number nine in a red circle," the Commander said.

"That wouldn't make sense if there were only five taken by the Shadow," said Oliver.

"It may add up if there were any taken last time the Shadow came through."

The Commander sent a sound message to one of the Hunters. "Bobby, look up how many were taken last time the shadow came through." *Pop.*

"Four, Commander. Taken five years ago." *Pop.*

"Gather the retrieval team," said the Commander.

Chapter 25

Flower Spirit

Monday, June 12, 1900

Rain pummeled the window of Dagur's house. Ella slammed shut the last dresser drawer in Dagur's room and kicked it for good measure. All she wanted in this moment was to find Megs. She was close — she could feel it on the edges of her Spirit. And yet, she had no next step. In fact, she had to meet Oliver and the Commander in Alveland at dinner time, which meant taking a step backwards, away from Megs. She was certain that Megs was in the human realm.

Now, she was in Mannland, and instead of searching for Megs, she had to search Dagur's house for more clues. She had to because it was an order from her superior Hunters. She and Haven searched systematically as they had been trained in Hunter school. Nevertheless, the papers in the desk were the only useful piece of information they had. It was eerie enough to be inside a human's house, and even eerier without the human there.

Ella did not know how to feel about those damn papers. They were undeniably incriminating, which made her desperately sad that Dagur was not who she thought he was. On the other hand, it was the surest way to intercept the prophecy and give the elvish race a fighting chance for survival. Ella still had the chills from Dagur's transformation. She had kissed Dagur, which made her insides squirm. Her feelings were a jumble of mess. She wanted to go back to Alveland; she needed a swim in her river.

Alveland would be abuzz today, preparing for tomorrow's festivities. Tomorrow was the Summer Solstice.

"What will you wear?" Haven asked.

"Hm?" Ella asked. She had been staring out the window at the rain.

"For the Solstice Celebration," Haven said.

Ella shrugged. She hadn't thought about the Solstice Celebration since they came to Mannland. In terms of dress, she had enough party dresses at her parents' house, to last her a long time, but now that she was a Huntress, she didn't think about dresses as much. Now, her closet was full of lineny pants and unembroidered shirts. Oddly enough, Ella was used to the pants and plain shirts, now. In fact, she preferred them. (The Hunter boots were still the ugliest things she'd ever seen — she would never prefer them. But they were admittedly practical.)

Ella looked down at her Mannland outfit. "Maybe I'll go to Aerilaya's when we get back to Alveland. Haven't been there since my broken engagement." Ella would rather go to Aerilaya's and buy herself a new dress with her currency, than go back to her old room. Part of her would be ashamed to do so, but part of her wasn't ready to revisit that place, yet. It would surely bring back memories from her life before Hunter school. And before Megs went missing. She missed Megs terribly.

Ella was so ready for Alveland.

"Is this a wrap?" Ella asked Haven.

"The human house is wrapped," Haven said.

The two lady-elves donned their elvish cloaks and left. As Ella stepped out of Dagur's front door and walked down the steps something caught her attention. It was the flower she had seen on their way inside. Beside it, grew another patch of ivy. It all felt like Megs. It felt like Megs strongly.

"Ells?" Haven said.

Ella followed the ivy vines, slowly at first.

"Where are you, Megs?" Ella broke into a run.

The ivy wove its way through the center of town.

"I thought we were going dress shopping," said Haven.

"Change of plans," said Ella.

———

"You've done this before?" Haven asked.

"Once. But the ivy stopped."

The two elves were both running, now. They ran through the empty afternoon streets of Reykjavik and down an alley. It led to a storage building and crept right under the back door.

Ella grabbed the doorknob.

"Wait," whispered Haven. "You can't just barge into a building in another realm."

Haven was right, of course. Ella needed to remember her training. Much more carefully, Ella tried the doorknob, keeping it quiet. It didn't budge. She tried to charm the lock, but without Alveland's energy supply it was difficult. Haven and Ella worked the charm together and the lock gave way.

Inside was darkness. Ella wished it was sunny instead of raining, so some of the light outdoors would shine into the building. Ella and Haven plastered their backs against the wall and followed it down a short hallway and down a flight of unlit stairs. With their elvish vision they could see a dirt floor below, and with their elvish hearing they could hear voices, too.

"Ella!"

"Megs?" Ella reached her hand through prison bars and grabbed her dear friend's hand.

"You found me, did you follow my ivy?" Megs said.

"I knew it was you," said Ella.

"I was calling to my Flower Spirit."

"But you're a Fire Spirit," Ella laughed.

"Would you have listened to the sconces?" Megs asked.

Ella covered a smile with her hand. She reminded herself that she was standing in the same room as Megs. She had known all along that Megs was alive, and she was right about her being trapped in Mannland. Now she needed to get Megs out of prison, along with the rest of the Missing. She began to examine the bars and the lock.

Something moved from the darkness to Ella's left.

"Look out!" Megs yelled, but it was too late. Ella and Haven were roughly grabbed by none other than Peter Burvanyek and a human whom Ella and Haven recognized. It was Jason, Dagur's friend who was obsessed with power. Ella didn't care for him that night she had met him at John Gregor's, and she was even less fond of him now.

Ella had almost regenerated her magic completely — it had been six days since her Total Exertion. Ella and Haven tried to shoot fire and spells at Burvanyek and Jason, but the block Burvanyek had around the two of them was so secure, Ella could not feel either of their essences through it. How could he have such strong magic in Mannland? Burvanyek and Jason locked both lass-elves in the musty, dank prison with the others and left without a word of explanation.

Ella had been engaged to the Prince. Then she became a Huntress. Now she was one of the Missing. Who would she be next?

———

"If I'd known they were there, I would have warned you," Megs said. "They usually leave during the day."

"Where do they go?" Ella asked.

Megs shrugged.

Ella and Haven, still soaking wet from the rain, used magic to pull the moisture from their hair and clothes. Ella introduced herself and Haven to the rest of the Missing. Then she and Megs wrapped each other in a hug and danced around in circles, squealing like piglets in the echoless prison cell. The other elves laughed at the dichotomic display of joy.

"Let me look at you." Megs held Ella at an arm's length.

Ella rolled her eyes.

"There's something different about you," Megs said.

Ella wondered how Megs could tell such things in a dark room in the basement of the human realm.

"She's a Hunteress," Haven said.

"No way," Megs said.

Ella nodded.

"By the Spirits. I am so proud of you," Megs said. "Is that how you found us?"

Ella nodded again.

"It was the only way I could think to find you," Ella said.

"It suits you," Megs said.

Ella beamed.

"Haven and I were spying in Mannland," Ella said.

"By yourselves?" Megs asked.

"No, with the Commander and Oliver," Ella said.

Megs gasped.

"What?" Ella asked.

"You love him," Megs said.

"Who?" Ella asked.

"Oliver," Megs said. "I can tell by the way you just said his name."

Ella gave Megs a bewildered look. "Right… sure…" Ella rolled her eyes and tried to dismiss Megs' comment with something sarcastic. Unfortunately, Ella couldn't seem to form a sentence. The way she felt about Oliver was surely different than the way she felt about anyone else. It was different from the way she felt about Emil or even Dagur.

"It's not like I…" Ella still couldn't say it. She knew why she couldn't deny her love for Oliver, too. She couldn't deny it because she loved Oliver with her emotions and with her brain and with parts of her Spirit that she didn't even know existed before she met him. How inconvenient for love to arise at a time like this.

Megs and Haven hid smiles.

Ella was annoyed.

"How can we be having a conversation about lad-elves in a place like this?" Ella burst out.

"You love him!" Megs said again.

"Fine!" Ella said. "I love him. Now, can we please figure out a way out of here?"

Ella tried to send a sound message to Oliver and the Commander, but it bounced off the prison walls and refused to travel. A sliver of firelight shone across Ella's eyes, waking her from her spot on the prison floor. She and Megs were sharing a bedroll. Their blanket was barely thin enough to keep them cold.

"Burvanyek will surely be back with the glass orbs," said Megs. "He forces everyone to Total Exert themselves and give him their energy."

That would certainly make it more difficult to escape on their own. Ella groaned. "But I just got my magic back after my last Total Exertion," she said. "Hopefully the Commander will be back with the key before Burvanyek returns with the orbs."

Chapter 26

Rescue

Tuesday, June 13, 1900

The hairs prickled on the back of Oliver's neck. Ella and Haven were supposed to have met them at the Commander's palace office at five o'clock. They needed to debrief and send out the retrieval team. It was now half past six. Oliver poured himself another glass of scotch. He needed something to do instead of wait. His father bustled around the office, pausing often to check the clock on the wall. It was ticking inordinately loudly. Neither of them tried to stop the red, anxious energy pulsing from them. They both knew that something was wrong. Surely one of them would have thought to send a sound message if they were going to be this late — unless something was preventing them from it. Images of Ella at the hands of more elvish oppressors in Mannland took over his brain and he couldn't think.

Oliver sloshed back the last swill of scotch and stood with such conviction that he knocked over the chair in which he was sitting. The Commander grabbed his cloak and Hunterpack and both elves left without hardly more than a glance at each other.

First, they rushed to the castle to retrieve Dagur from the dungeon. They may have need of him once they return to Mannland. Commander Agnarsson and General Agnarsson deployed the retrieval team by sound message, giving them orders to travel through Mannland in pairs, and not a crowd. Then, they followed the crudely drawn map found in Dagur's desk drawer. By seven-thirty, they had hurried through Reykjavik and were on the other side of the city.

Oliver had to stop himself from traveling at a highly conspicuous elvish run. He had to get to Ella, and he hoped that she was hidden on the spot where he was going. If he was hurrying to this spot, and she wasn't there, he may lose control of himself. He was barely holding in his energies and fears as it was.

Finally, the map led them to a ramshackle storage building. It lay in an unlit alley. The thought of Ella being in a place like this gave Oliver a chill. By the Spirits, let him find her, and let her be okay.

Oliver and the Commander lay their hands against the door, scanning for elvish energy, danger and anything else useful. There were definitely elves behind the door, though the energy level was faint. The eight members of the retrieval team lay in wait around the side of the building.

At the Commander's signal, Oliver cast off the lock from the back door. He and the Commander traveled, backs to the wall, down a set of stairs and toward the faint elvish energy in the room below.

When he saw Ella, he ran to her and reached his arm through the bars until they were ripping at his shoulder flesh. She met him and he was able to touch the soft skin on her face. The sight of her in danger made Oliver's heart ache.

"How do we get them out?" Oliver's voice was more of a growl than speech. His question was addressed more to his anger than to a person.

"Howdy," Megs said.

Oliver stared at the lass-elf for a beat before realizing who it was. The person who spurred Ella's mission. "Megs," Oliver greeted.

Ella wrapped an arm around her friend's shoulders and smiled. How could Megs be sarcastic and Ella be smiling at a time like this. They were in danger.

"Can we focus, please?" Oliver affixed his face with what he hoped was a particularly menacing glower. It wasn't difficult, as it was how he felt.

Ella and Megs looked at each other and smirked.

Oliver chose to ignore them, and try to break the lock. It was blocked by magic, of course. Oliver hadn't expected to be able to open the door so easily, but he had to try. Oliver began searching around the edges of the bars, desperate to locate another way to break in.

"General," the Commander said.

"Sir." Oliver stopped his frantic search and faced him. He just knew he was going to say something he didn't want to hear.

"Return to the oppressor's house, and search the desk for a key. I'll remain with the prisoners," Commander Agnarsson said.

"Sir." Oliver was desperate to stay with Ella, but he wouldn't defy his father. Not after all he'd been through to restore their relationship. He looked desperately from Ella to the Commander.

"General," the Commander said again. "After further consideration, I'd like to order you to guard the prisoners, while I retrieve the key."

Oliver exhaled with relief and immediately turned to Ella at the prison door.

"Commander," Oliver said. "Thank you, sir."

The Commander nodded.

"Sir," Oliver said again. "Take the human. He may be useful in helping you find the key."

"Agreed," the Commander said.

Dagur left with the Commander, and Oliver turned back to Ella once more.

"Best day," Oliver said.

"Best day," Ella answered.

There was a beat of silence before all the elves in the basement laughed at the ridiculousness of the optimistic elvish greeting. It definitely hadn't been the best day.

"Are you okay?" Oliver asked. "Are you hurt?"

"Fine, thank you," Ella said. "Look, though. I found Megs."

"Well done," Oliver said. "Perhaps next time you could find the Missing without becoming one of the Missing yourself."

Ella gave Oliver a deadpan look. "It was my first Hunter rescue. Surely you wouldn't expect me to do it perfectly."

Oliver opened his mouth to argue, but Ella interrupted.

"Listen. It's Burvanyek. He's working with a human named Jason. Jason is friends with Dagur. Or enemies, or something. They know each other."

"And we don't have any magic," Ella continued. "None of the Missing does. He had us exercise Total Exertion into an orb."

Oliver furrowed his brow, confused.

"He takes the magic from the orb and uses it for himself. Every week."

"He has all the energy from all of you each week?" Oliver's voice sounded incredulous. "That would make him…"

"Powerful," said Ella. "Undefeatable."

Oliver raked his fingers through his hair. This was a predicament. "If one elf had his own power, plus the power of five elves on a weekly basis…"

"We think he has more strongholds like this one in other lands, too," Ella said.

Oliver huffed out the last of his air and sat against the wall. This was more than a predicament. If he, Ohghee and Klayden had an unending supply of energy, they would be indestructible.

"Oliver," Ella said. His name sounded musical coming from her lips. "If Burvanyek comes back, you have to escape. When he sees you, he'll try to kill you."

"I can't leave without you," Oliver said. Then added, "And the Missing."

"You can come back for us," Ella said.

Oliver doubted he'd be able to drag himself from Ella's side, even though what she was saying made sense. Oliver waited with the Missing. He had the rest of the retrieval team outside on lookout. They all hoped that the Commander would return before Burvanyek, which he did — sort of. The door opened, and Dagur entered. His father must have sent him ahead in case Burvanyek had arrived first. Two retrievers, Darren and Gilmer, escorted him downstairs.

Ella wandered over to him. "Why?" she asked. "Why are you working for Peter Burvanyek?"

Dagur considered the question. It seemed like he was trying to figure out whether or not to answer truthfully. "I'm working for the resistance, with Jason. Without help, the resistance will fail. Burvanyek can give us more power than we need."

"Your government is peaceful," Ella argued. "You don't need him."

Dagur looked away. "My courtship of you was real," Dagur said. "Not that it matters, now."

"Certainly not now that you're an elvish oppressor," Ella said.

"I don't suppose you'd come away with me if I weren't an elvish oppressor."

Oliver wanted to know the answer to that question as well, but Ella didn't have time to answer.

The door smashed open at the top of the stairs.

"General!" Darren called down to him, alerting him of danger. Peter Burvanyek had returned. Oliver darted up the stairs and hid in the corner of the landing.

"You," Burvanyek said when he saw Dagur. Oliver knew Burvanyek suspected treason. Burvanyek ran down the stairs, brushing by Oliver's hiding spot. When he stood before Dagur, Burvanyek shot a spell at him from the palm of his hand. Dagur slumped against the wall, dead. Ella and Megs both held in screams.

Because Burvanyek hadn't been alerted to Oliver's presence, Oliver may have a chance at escape. If Burvanyek knew he was there, he'd already be dead. Oliver shot a particularly brutal charm at Peter's face. Anyone else probably would have been dead, but since Peter was running on the stolen magic of dozens of elves, he bounced back fairly quickly — too quickly. Oliver dove through the doorway and Burvanyek shot a spell at him. Oliver tore through town, running helter-skelter though

Reykjavik center. The retrieval team came into play. Darren and Gilmer flanked Oliver while the other six faced Burvanyek. Oliver hoped to the Spirits all the elves would all make it back to Alveland, where they belonged. As Oliver traveled through the buildings of Reykjavik at an elvish run, Oliver knew Burvanyek was following. Oliver could feel it.

Ella called to the Spirits, far away in Alveland to protect Oliver. Soon after Burvanyek chased Oliver from the prison room, the Commander arrived with the key. He unlocked the door to the prison cell, and the Missing elves escaped. It pained Ella to leave Dagur's lifeless body. It would probably be discovered later that day by Jason. The elves nervously traveled through town, waiting to be attacked by Burvanyek at any moment. Ella hoped to the Spirits that she wouldn't find Oliver's body somewhere along their pathway back to the elvish realm. By Alveland, let him get through the portal safely.

Chapter 27

One Wild Night

Wednesday, June 21, 1900

Summer Solstice, already a wild night of celebration and shenanigans, had a rare electricity about it surrounding the joy of the return of the Missing. Ella supposed that now, they could be referred to as the Found. Last week, Ella and the Commander were relieved to find Oliver waiting for them all on the other side of the portal door.

Ella, Haven and the Commander took Oliver and all of the Missing to the Healer who attended to them. Ella had forgotten how old the Healer was. The skin on her face was leathery, still beautiful, but leathery. Her crimped gray hair reached to her knees and hung in the folds of her linen, elvish garments. Ella wondered when she would take her final journey into the mountains. After their examinations, the Healer sent the Hunters and the Found home to their families for a loving recovery.

Today, the elves of Alveland prepared for the Solstice feast. Beginning early in the morning, the elves began turning themselves into a work of art. They gathered costumes, body paint, and more. However, the Hunters also packed their Hunterpacks. They needed to be ready for a fight. Burvanyek was still looking for an entrance to their portal, and the Shadow was hovering off the coast in the Snolandic Sea. The trackers could feel its constant, looming presence. Indeed, there was a nervousness that contributed to the electrically-charged Solstice atmosphere.

Having woken up safely in the Amarind Building this morning, with Megs camping out in her dorm, Ella decided to go to Aerilaya's. She purchased a simple black dress. It hugged her hips and fell all the way to the floor in one, sleek sheath. Without Mitsy to steam it for her, she hung it in her room and sprayed it with lavender water to release the wrinkles. With the sun setting slowly behind the palace, Ella did her face paint, white and cloudy, with fierce black liner on her eyes. Last, she added her white fox skin atop teased curls.

She looked positively wild — as she should for Eina Villta Nótt, or 'One Wild Night'.

Eina Villta Nótt was the other name for the grand celebration of the Summer Solstice. For sheer joy, Ella, Megs and Haven chose to take the Fainde River ferry to the celebration. Before the ferry docked, she could already see the massive bonfire raging in the dusk.

Ella looked at her friends' Solstice attire out of the corner of her eye. Haven, like Ella wore a black dress. The neck was high, and wrapped closely around her neck. Haven had also painted black onto her face, chest and arms. Atop her head was an angry crow head. Only the whites of Haven's eyes and her smiling teeth could be seen. The outfit was just right for Haven's bold Spirit.

Megs, of course, had the most unique outfit. Her ceremonial dress was bright red to go with her red fox headpiece. She wanted to be a fox in order to complement Ella, but of course needed her own flare. She created beautiful temporary red tattoos up and down her arms and legs. It took her most of the morning.

Ella was happy to be Megs' right-hand fox. Ella so admired foxes. She was convinced that they were the happiest of the woodland creatures. They were big enough to be predators to most, and clever enough to escape their predators. And their fur. Ella thought if she was really a fox, she might spend all day staring at her own reflection in the river, admiring the soft sheen. And Ella especially admired the rare beauty of white foxes.

As the ferry docked, Ella could hardly wait to deboard and run to the celebration. All of the elves in the Palace Province were descending upon the flatlands next to the palace. Upon arrival, she met her parents. When Ella was hugged by her mother, she thought that her mother might never let go.

"We heard about your spying mission in Mannland," her mother said.

Ella nodded.

Both of her parents crossed their fists across their chest and bowed in their elvish sign of respect. Ella returned the gesture.

"We're so proud of you," her father said.

"And your Solstice dress is..." Mrs Marina's sentence trailed off as she hid her smile behind her hand. Ella could see the pride in her mother's eyes. It was like she could finally see Ella for the lady-elf she had become.

Ella lifted her skirt and did a spin, sending her fern flower necklace flying into the air before it rested again between her breasts. With joy bubbling in her heart and out into the air around her, she got to introduce some of her favorite people to each other: She introduced Haven Rae to her parents. And her parents spent a great deal of time fawning over Megs' return.

When everyone was introduced, Ella, Megs and Haven walked around the festival. Magic filled the air with palpable joy. Ella detected the scent of Hotasoley Avens and Arctic Thyme and her Spirit soared. As the three lady-elves wove their way through the crowds, they linked pinky fingers in sisterly solidarity, the energy from all three weaving in and out of them. As they walked, Ella felt a tug on her black dress.

Kristin stood next to her, dressed as an arctic hare. Her white dress tied at the shoulders and was covered in eyelets. Atop her head were two white bunny ears, positioned at an angle. Ella crouched down to Kristin's level.

"You look beautiful tonight," Ella whispered to the shy lass-elf.

Kristin held up her hands to show Ella a fluffy white puff of cuteness. "Looka me bonded an'mal," Kristin said.

Ella gasped. It was a preciously cute arctic fox cub — the perfect bonded animal for sweet Kristin. And it matched Ella's Solstice costume. "Can I pet her?" Ella asked.

"Uh huh," Kristin said.

The cub whined curiously.

"What will you name her?" Ella asked.

"Solley Villa," said Kristin.

The perfect name for a fox cub, the color of a Hotasoley, bonded on Eina Villta Nótt.

Kristin leaned over to Ella to whisper something in her ear.

"I hope you get the fern flower," Kristin said.

Ella felt her nomination necklace around her neck. It had started to glow with the sunset, and now shone blue against her outfit. "Thank you," Ella said. "I'm sure Alveland will give it to the one of us who needs it the most." Ella didn't know. After Emil had broken their engagement and the Shadow had attacked, she would have been certain that Alveland would bestow its blessing of abundance on her. Now, however, she felt fairly supplied with her own abundance, so she simply trusted in Alveland's wisdom for the gift — as it should have been all along.

Kristin returned to her family. Ella waved to them from across the crowd. Haven and Megs, who had disappeared during Ella's conversation with Kristin, returned with firecrackers — not the flammable kind, the beverage. Haven counted down from three and they all drank their shots. It burned like fire, hence the name.

A low drum beat began across the crowd, on the other side of the circle. Torches flew up and moved toward the fire. Most of the lad-elves had created fire, lit torches and began the traditional Eina Villta Nótt dance. Megs and Ella stood next to each other and admired it. The dance was strong and fierce, and Ella felt the beat of the drum in her body. The men moved around the circle.

Oliver crossed in front of them and Ella forgot how to breathe. He was shirtless, as were most of the lads. He wore black trousers and a matching black wolf head on top of his own. The face was fixed in a snarl. It was the most perfect Eina Villta Nótt ensemble for a Hunter General. Across his chest, he had drawn black lines to look like claw marks. His gaze met hers for a fraction of a second, and Ella felt drawn to him. She grabbed onto Megs' shoulder to ground herself. Megs poked her in the ribs and Ella blushed furiously.

———

Oliver blended into the crowd.

The drum beat slowed and a wooden flute joined it, beginning the dance for the lady-elves. He couldn't stop himself from looking for Ella. The dance was seductive and fluid. They spun around the circle, occasionally pausing to snap their hands above their heads. With each snap, a little flame was released from their palms.

He finally spotted Ella. When he did, he felt a pull behind his navel. He willed himself to stay where he was. She moved behind the great bonfire, and Oliver felt frustrated when he lost sight of her.

After the dancing, the formal part of the ceremony began. First, the Royal Council spoke. One of the Royal Advisors welcomed everyone. Then, the Keeper told the legend of Princess Kari and the fern flower. As they did so, Ella moved forward, toward the presenters along with the other nine nominees.

"Kari was a lass-elf, about ninety-four (seventeen) years old. She loved to be by the fjords and feed her ocean Spirit. She loved to listen to the crashing surf and feel the mysterious sea mist against her face. One day she was kidnapped by Milgren the troll, one who had always hated the joy and beauty of the elves. The black-hearted troll kept Kari locked up on his island and treated her with unspeakable harshness. Kari's family, not knowing about the kidnapping, looked for her on the fjord and in the sea for years. They were finally forced to give up and assume that the Snolandic Sea had claimed Kari for its own.

"Years later, a royal ship discovered Kari's island. The Prince of Alveland, Prince Jerome, was an adventurer and he gathered a crew to go sailing the sea. When he came ashore to explore the island, he discovered Kari in one of the troll's caves along the rocky cliffs. When Prince Jerome saw Kari, waves of turquoise and yellow energy emerged from him and he knew that he needed to save Kari and make her his Princess.

"So Prince Jerome dared to rescue her. First, he had to retrieve an axe from his ship to break her chains. She was weak with hunger, so the kind, young Prince carried his love aboard the royal ship.

"Unfortunately, as they were leaving the island, the troll arrived at the cave and discovered Kari's absence. The troll pursued them. The Prince docked in the harbor and deboarded his royal crew. But as they did, they watched the troll steer his boat into the fjord. Once on land, Prince Jerome gathered the Hunters and prepared to fight. But the troll was not witless. From the deck of his boat, before he even docked, the troll challenged Prince Jerome to a duel.

"If the troll had come on land, he would have been destroyed by the elvish Hunters. Outnumbered and out skilled. However, a duel would mean a fight with only strength between two single beings. To refuse a duel was cowardly — Prince Jerome had to fight the troll for the safety of Kari and to avoid a war between trolls and elves.

"Prince Jerome agreed to the fight and waited for the troll to dock his ship. While he waited, he carried Kari to the Healer. So the story goes, as the Prince and Kari traveled inland, a mysterious glow shone along their path. It was the Alveland fern flower — only heard of until then.

"When Kari and the Prince stepped into the flower's glow, the troll ran his boat against a rock in the fjord and drowned. With the help of the fern flower, Kari and the Prince married. Alveland blessed them with many children in order to heal Kari's heart and bring her joy to make up for the years she suffered at the hands of Milgren the troll.

"So they say, those elves who have more than one child are rumored to be descendants of the strong, long-suffering Princess Kari. And to the elves' delight, the fern flower has bloomed each year on the night of the Summer Solstice to bring great blessing to the Aveland chosen elf."

After his story, the Keeper reached his hands out over the nine assembled nominees and blessed them in their search for the fern flower.

The last organized event of the evening was the ritual sacrifice. The Royal Council threw one of the Council's young children into the river, squealing with delight, as the summer's sacrifice to nature. All the other young children were jealous that they didn't get to be the sacrifice, so they all jumped in, too. They were sure to play there for the remainder of the evening, splashing and laughing.

Usually music and dancing followed the summer sacrifice, but to everyone's surprise, King Frederick spoke. A stillness came over the crowd as they craned their necks and ears to his speech.

"Good elves," the King said. "An announcement I must make, though I don't want to on this night of celebration. We have confirmed what we have suspected for years, that Peter Burvanyek is, in fact, trying to gain rule in Mannland. We believe he is working as a member of the Wicked Three. And we believe they are behind the Shadow, which is scheduled to return any time. We refuse to let it ruin our celebration or interfere with our traditions. If it does in fact arrive as expected, we will take shelter as before, and rebuild as necessary when it leaves. Hunters, be ready to report and fight at first sign." There was a moment of silence and sadness and respect for the King.

After the King's announcement, several musicians began to play. First the low drum, followed by the wooden flutes and an assortment of percussion. Oliver put his hands in his pockets. He didn't really want to dance, again. Not unless it was with Ella. And he wasn't sure that was a good idea. When she went missing yesterday, his stomach was in knots. And yet, he didn't feel like he was in the wrong place, protecting Alveland from the elvish oppressor, Dagur. For the first time, he felt like he could understand his parents and his childhood. They loved him, yet they also were made complete by defending Alveland as Hunters. Maybe he could finally forgive his father for the wee version of himself.

He looked up from the fire and saw Ella. She was dancing with Haven and Megs, spinning until they were dizzy, as the dance steps called for. She was laughing in her freely joyful way with her platinum curls flying wildly. Oliver took a step towards her. He had never dealt with his love for Ella except to suppress it with the strongest energy blocks he could muster. She had been engaged to the Prince all these years, and he had been a Hunter. She would never have understood. No one would have understood.

But now, she was a Huntress. They had completed a mission in Mannland together. She had sacrificed for Alveland in a similar way. Oliver wondered if she would continue in being a Hunter, training fighters in Glima and accepting missions from the Commander now that Megs was back. It wasn't unusual for Hunters and Hunteresses to change vocations after a time. Hunting was an incredibly high honor status in Alveland, but it was also full of intense sacrifice, and sometimes elves needed a break from that to live a normal life in Alveland.

Oliver took another step toward Ella. She was a Hunteress, and Emil had chosen another suitor. For the first time in his elvish life, hope bubbled in his chest. It was an unfamiliar feeling. Before he knew how, Oliver was right next to Ella.

She spun away from Megs and Haven and landed in his arms. Ella looked horrified to see him. She didn't move until Megs ran up behind her and gave her a shove.

With Ella in his arms, Oliver led her around the bonfire, dancing with other elves. This was a special night. Oliver wanted to make Ella happy, and her dimple told him that she was. The firelight cast shadows across Ella's already painted face and it sent a quiver through his elvish body. When the musicians took a break for refreshment, Ella returned to Megs and Haven, and Oliver returned to the shadows, alone.

He attended a feast table, packed with all matters of colorful food. In the center was a bowl of Solstice Punch — something appropriate for the children — as well as a second bowl of Solstice Brew which could punch any grown lad or lady-elf in the guts. He tried a taste of the brew and then decided on filling his drinking chalice with the punch. After all, he needed to have his wits about him if the Shadow arrived soon. He had received several sound messages from his father who was somewhere amidst the celebration. He reported that the trackers had tracked the Shadow recently, and it was poised and hovering off the coast in the Snolandic Sea.

A short and darkly dressed bear ran over to the table and grabbed a handful of food off the table for himself and his Slow Loris. Oliver recognized him as Gunnar, one of Ella's charges.

"General Agnarsson." Gunnar crossed his fist across his chest and bowed to Oliver who returned the gesture. "Best day."

"Best day," Oliver said.

Neither lad-elf knew what to say to each other, so they nodded respectfully.

"Trees are useful…" Oliver said.

It was an odd thing to say, but it held Gunnar's attention.

"…for sending off your anger," Oliver said.

Gunnar furrowed his brow.

Oliver walked behind the table to the edge of the forest and placed a hand along the trunk of a crepe myrtle.

"Your parents love you," Oliver said. "And you are serving Alveland simply by being their son."

Oliver located some of his lurking anger, residing just behind his navel and sent it into the tree with a satisfying zap. Oliver and Gunnar watched the tree whisk it down, below the earth and felt it surge through its roots and away forever. Gunnar nodded to Oliver one last time before charging off into the night to rejoin the fun. Oliver left his chalice on the table, and headed north-east toward the Fainde River Bridge.

Oliver had held Ella's body with a strong hand, and led her securely in the dances they had been doing their whole lives. As usual, he smelled like the ocean, which calmed her, and his nearness made her cheeks feel hot. She decided that if she could have been anywhere in the entire world, it would have been right there.

The Shadow was near. Ella had heard that from Haven, who had received a sound message from Commander Agnarsson. Ella stepped away from the celebration, if only briefly. She needed comfort and a recharge for any fight that may be coming this way. She needed her river.

When she arrived, she heard the children playing in the water, so she took the quieter route to the river, over the bridge. She was only slightly surprised to see Oliver there. They had both had a thing for the river since they were small. He was leaning on the bridge and looking out at the quiet ripples and dribbling rapids. Ella leaned against the bridge right next to him, and the two enjoyed the river in silence.

"You're a good fighter," Oliver said.

That was a bit of a disappointing start to the conversation Ella wanted to have with the lad-elf she loved. "Thank you," she said.

"It's been a significant year," said Oliver.

"It's been over a hundred years, for us." Ella's dimple appeared, thinking of the vast expanse of time she'd known Oliver.

"The Shadow," Oliver said.

"And Megs,"

"And the Hunters."

"And Glima."

Oliver and Ella had both taken off their Solstice headpieces. Looking at him, now, his hair was spiky and he looked the part of a dangerous Hunter. If she were the enemy, she'd be terrified of him. His black, elvish chalk paint defined his muscles in the best way. The sconces at the edge of the bridge flickered, and from a distance, they could hear the night's musicians begin their last set of the night. The hand drum began a lazy beat and the accordion joined with a lilting melody. Ella's elation made her head spin, and she stopped trying not to smile. She wiggled her feet in her shoes to celebrate.

When Oliver wrapped his arms around her, Ella's stomach did a flip-flop.

Oliver pulled her close and hummed low and deep. The stress in her shoulders slid down her arms and the sadness in her stomach untied. She felt Oliver's soothing spell working well on her. It was the same kind of spell her mother used on her when she was a little girl and she was upset. The knots Oliver was untying were much more tightly tied than the ones her mother had helped her with. She felt better as peace replaced the knots. When he stopped humming, all that was left was the joy of the Summer Solstice. She allowed that yellow energy to pour out of her and disappear over the bridge.

Oliver tilted Ella's chin towards him and studied her mouth in the darkness. The electricity from the celebration, the magic of the elves and maroon energy from two elves on the bridge mingled around them until they felt alone. Ella's heart raced with anticipation as she waited. Finally, Oliver leaned down and pressed a gentle kiss against Ella's lips. Ella had never experienced such a kiss. She wasn't sure that anyone had experienced such a kiss, or if anyone would ever experience such a kiss again.

She hoped to the Spirits that it wouldn't have to end. Ella tried to talk some sense into herself by reminding herself that Oliver was probably just using her as a distraction. He tended to use lots of lass-elves as distractions from whatever he was angry about. Unfortunately, the kiss had meant something to Ella. She loved Oliver, and she was okay with that. It probably wasn't a good idea to tell him, though, because he surely didn't love her back. Her heart could take a lot of things, apparently, but she thought she'd like to save this last, particular part of her heart from rejection. Their kiss did end eventually, and it did when the Commander's voice arrived in a sound message.

"Report to the palace courtyard." *Pop.*

Chapter 28

Shadow Returns

Wednesday, June 21, 1900

Oliver grabbed Ella's hand and the two of them ran toward the palace. The celebration had quieted, yet the elves did not raise chaos. They passed Megs and Ella's parents. Ella hugged them all and sent them off together this time to the Marina's house. Ella sent ShaSha with Megs and Dietze.

Next, they passed the Holding family.

"We must go," Lady Hilda said to her husband.

"We can't both go," Sir Vincent said. "What about the children?"

"Send Andri and Kristin home with Gunnar," Ella placed her hand gently on Lady Hilda's shoulder. "He can handle it."

Gunnar tucked his hoverboard under his arm and grasped the hands of his little siblings. He looked around at his parents, Oliver and Ella, and nodded. A great sense of purpose filled his eyes. Hilda kissed his cheek and sent her three children off together toward their home .

"May the Spirits protect them," Hilda said.

"May they protect us all," Ella said.

The two Advisors and the two Hunters made their way to the palace. Ella made herself ready. She met with the Hunter women in a Great Room of the palace to change into her Hunter clothes. She wiped off most of her face paint, but kept the fierce eye circles. Then, she braided her blonde hair back so it would be out of her way for fighting.

They had been trained for this. The Hunters left all of their belongings except for the Hunterpacks filled with weapons and rations and exited out the front door of the palace. Ella felt the chill. That same, terrible, debilitating chill that she felt that day outside of Marilla's when Megs was taken. She saw the Shadow rise up and over the dwellings and move closer to the palace. Ella vomited, which made her feel weak. But she did not run this time. She stayed with the larger group of Hunters, and walked steadily towards the Shadow. Several groups of Hunters left the group in order to aid royal elves and elves in trouble. They must protect their population.

But Ella marched on. The Shadow covered the first group of Hunters. Cries rose up from the darkness. Others dove to the side in order to let it pass beside them. She caught sight of Commander Agnarsson and Oliver up ahead, moving elves aside to safety and marching toward the Shadow. Ella had to decide. Should she stay and be covered by the Shadow? Maybe taken? Or should she dodge it in hopes of being able to help other elves survive the attack. In training, it had been clear that this was always a Hunter's choice. Either was noble. Either was probably as unproductive as the other. There was always the chance that a Hunter would learn something new if they stayed within the Shadow, but so far that was untrue. Their training always emphasized ways to conserve energy until after the attack. Energy would be required to save others, rebuild Alveland or participate in a team.

Ella stopped walking and looked at the Shadow, pondering it. Maybe it was time to try something different. Ella set down her Hunterpack.

"Oliver!" Ella wasn't sure why she called out his name, but he turned around and locked eyes with her. He ran towards her, and she knew that he would save her again. She knew that he would whisk her away to Mannland again, if necessary. But that wasn't her intention at all. The Shadow was less than a yard away from her. She lifted her arms out to the side and Totally Exerted herself. All of the elves surrounding her, both Hunters and non, were blown over by the force of the magic. Ella felt the lightning in her arms and heard the whistle of the wind as all of her magic left her in all directions. She aimed both of her arms in front of her at the Shadow and it blew back like a cloud. It rolled and rolled back toward the sea. It rolled and rolled back toward town. Past Marilla's. Ella's magic shook the ground and all the elves covered their heads until the minutes were up and Ella stood weakly in the field, empty of magic.

But there, just in front of town, just in front of the Shadow's edge crouched a figure. A figure that everyone recognized. There on the ground before them was Ohghee, the leader of the Wicked Three.

Celvin jumped to his feet, and with a great shout from his guts practiced Total Exertion like Ella. His magic rolled the Shadow back closer to the sea. The TE left all the elves rooted to their spots, taking cover with their hands and Hunterpacks as his magic flew over the land. When his minutes were up, Ella looked up from her spot on the ground. There, in the space behind Ohghee, sat Klayden, the second member of the Wicked Three.

"One more," whispered Ella, from her spot against the earth.

Haven did it. She Totally Exerted herself and revealed Peter Burvanyek, who had obviously found his way back into Alveland.

"No more!" shouted the Commander. It wasn't out of anger. It was because they had achieved it. They had discovered the source of the Shadow. They had exposed the Wicked Three. The Wicked Three stood and moved together. They looked unphased, and the Shadow began to reconvene above their heads. They began their trek toward the palace, and Ella began to worry. She was out of ideas, had acted impulsively and was out of magic. And the Palace Province was still under attack.

―

The Wicked Three marched on toward the palace. The Shadow descended toward them, about to cover them again so they could resume their anonymous attack of terror.

"I challenge Ohghee to a duel," Ella heard herself say from her spot on the ground. She stood up and he turned to meet her gaze. Ella felt like her spirit was being sucked right out of her body as she looked in his face.

"No," yelled Oliver.

"Name your terms," said Ohghee. He held up his hand and held the Shadow at bay, hovering just above his head.

"Fighting, no magic," Ella said, since she had exerted all her magic.

"Done," said Ohghee.

"This cannot happen," Oliver said to the Hunters, who had created a summit. The war had been moved to the rocky shore. The Shadow was held out over the now frozen Snolandic Sea. The King, his Advisors, the Hunters, and the Palace Province people gathered by the foothills, and the Wicked Three gathered by town.

"It is the way for us to avoid a war," said Ella. "I shall fight instead of the entire province being sucked of life."

"You shall not fight. Ohghee will cheat. He will use magic."

Ella shrugged. "You don't know that."

"I do."

"It avoids war."

"It gets you killed."

"It is already done," Ella said.

She was not wrong. A challenged duel could not be avoided. It must be played out to death or defeat.

Commander Agnarsson did not argue with Ella. Neither did the King or the Prince.

Ohghee walked toward the province elves and marked a cross in the earth halfway between them, and waited for Ella.

Chapter 29

The Biggest Glima Match

Wednesday, June 21, 1900

Ella met him there and looked into the face of evil. His chestnut eyes looked like two stones that had sunk to the bottom of the sea. She looked into his spiritless eyes and grabbed forearms with Ohghee. She dug her feet into the earth, drawing in energy. Looking at her opponent, she analyzed him down to his muscle sinews. He was not especially tall, but stocky with strength. His hair, which was oddly well cared for, was tied back in a ponytail at the back of his neck. The short mustache and beard around his chin was too neatly trimmed for her to use it against him in a fight. She had chosen her moves and he had seen her win. Ohghee began their footwork, but Ella attacked first. When she grabbed for Ohghee, he came at her with such speed and force that Ella was unable to respond. Ella found herself stuck in a hold.

Damnit, thought Ella.

Ohghee exhaled and sent Ella hurtling to the earth. Since they were so close to the cliffs, the rocks and shells in the ground cut her back. It hurt terribly, and Ella drew in healing energy from the ground. Still feeling weak from her Total Exertion, Ella twisted away from a pin down. She leaped to her feet and started circling again. Ella was horrified to discover that Ohghee was a great Glima fighter.

Ella planned a risky takedown. She played out the step sequence in her mind. Ella grabbed Ohghee's hand and yanked it down. Then, she reached for Ohghee's face with a bird-claw hand. However, so Ohghee would not have the opportunity to pivot away, she stepped directly behind his foot. With one hand pulling his hand and one hand pushing his face and nowhere to step, Ohghee hit the earth with a finite thud. Ella backed away the victor.

Ella watched Ohghee get up. His face was fixed in a snarl. Ella was afraid to approach him, even to grab forearms, but she took a deep breath and did it anyway. Gray hatred oozed out of Ohghee's body. He didn't even try to control it. In fact, it clouded the air around them, so Ella couldn't even see him properly.

They each had a takedown. Whichever of them reached three takedowns won.

Ella got a weird feeling of warning from Alveland. It entered her body from the ground. What was it? Ohghee made the first attack and grabbed Ella on the bicep and back of the neck. Ella knew that twisting into the hold was the only way to get out of it. She tucked herself under Ohghee's arm and popped up behind him. Unfortunately, in the gray smoke, none of the other elves could see

Ohghee use magic. He sent a spell of pain through Ella so brutal that she fell backwards out of the smoke and onto her back once again. Without Ohghee's hands on her, the crowd could see that she had taken down herself, and Ohghee was the victor. He had two takedowns.

Ella didn't get up. It hadn't been a pain spell. It had been a death spell. She could feel the life leaving her as well as she could feel the pain in her stomach growing. She turned on her side, facing the sea so she could protect her midsection. Ohghee had never meant to fight fairly. Oliver knew that. Ella might have known that, too, but she didn't regret her choice. She would have made that sacrifice for Alveland again. Killing an elf didn't mean a thing to Ohghee. Ella heard a wave crash against the cliffs and she thought of Oliver. A tear left her eye as life left her body. As if summoned by her thoughts, Oliver appeared at her side.

"No," he whispered.

Ella shivered. She grew so cold as she died there on the ground by the sea.

Oliver pressed himself up against her back, engulfing her with his large frame, trying to keep her warm. "Someone help her! Healer! Keeper! Father!" Oliver took Ella's hand.

"I love you," he whispered in her ear. "I have loved you for twenty-seven years, and I'll love you for the rest of my life, until I become part of Alveland, and then my love for you will become a part of our people."

Because of Ella's fatal injuries, she could no longer speak. Nor could she let out her energies to show Oliver the joy she felt at his declaration. She could barely get in a breath. She desperately wanted to tell Oliver how much she loved him too. She patted the ground next to her head. A single, white Hotasoley blossom sprouted and bloomed from the earth. It matched the blossom she had sent out to sea for Oliver's mother on the Winter Solstice. One of its petals had a drop of Ella's blood in an aura of pink and maroon energies.

Oliver's tears fell on Ella's skin as she grew paler and paler. "No," Oliver said again. He looked up at the Healer, the Keeper, the King and his father, all surrounding them. "Do something!" he shouted at them angrily.

The Keeper looked behind Oliver and his eyes grew wide. "Look…"

A blue glow rose up from the ground by Ella's Hotasoley. A great warmth emanated from it as the great fern flower of Alveland rose up from the ground and into view. It had a dark, seeded center and stood nearly a yard high. Skinny leaves poked up all around the plant. Ella's glowing fern flower necklace glowed even brighter blue as the magic of Alveland flowed into Ella's limp and near-lifeless body. It pulsed through her until she was full of light. The flower remained aglow as well.

Ella sat up. She was able to stand and flex her muscles. She was healed — better than healed. She was strong with the grace of Alveland. Ella returned to the Glima cross and faced Ohghee. She had two more takedowns to execute. And finally, Ohghee looked properly nervous to be facing Alveland's greatest Glima champion.

"No," Oliver said. He grabbed Ella's hand. "Let me fight." Oliver's last demand was to Ohghee.

"No," said Ella. "This is my fight." She brought Oliver's fingers to her lips and kissed them before she turned back to Ohghee.

Ella attacked first. She got Ohghee in a throw down hold at his neck. He grabbed her hand and tried to curse her again, but she exerted a shield with her newfound Alveland magic. The spell backfired and seeped into his own skin. Ella threw him down.

The life began to leave Ohghee. His sallow face began to grow even more gaunt. He stepped away from the cross and drew life from Alveland. Lots of life. Too much life. The grass withered, the rocks melted, the plants and birds died all around them. Ohghee's squirrel tzi ran from him, but couldn't escape Ohghee's selfish grab of magic. Ohghee looked across the hill and watched his own tzi writhe and cry until it died.

Ella felt sick. How could an elf kill their own bonded animal? Ella felt her connection to the fern flower. It filled her with unending pulses of magic. Adrenaline pulsed through her. Ella glanced at the Palace Province elves, the King, the Healer, the Keeper. She looked at Haven and

Oliver. Ella had a lot to live for, and a lot to love, and she wasn't about to let some tzi killing wicked elf destroy what was hers.

She called to the Spirits, the fern flower and Alveland itself and stood by the cross. When she grabbed forearms with Ohghee his touch made her queasy. She had one more takedown in the biggest Glima match of her life.

Thud.

Ella had taken down Ohghee with a single hand. She hadn't even moved her feet. It was like her sheer will had been enough to destroy him forever. All of Alveland watched as Ohghee's stolen elvish magic left him and he died from his own spell. Quicker than a Taerry Dragon, Klayden and Burvanyek reached above them and submerged themselves in the mysterious covering of the Shadow. A gust of wind rushed across the land as the Shadow traveled out to sea.

Chapter 30

Grateful

Five Human Years Later…

Ella performed an under the throat drag down on Celvin. He landed with a thud, and Ella pinned his arms to his side and backed away for the victory. It was a common occurrence at Marilla's these days, seeing as how Ella was made an honorary teacher at Hunter University. She taught all new Hunter recruits Glima with the assistance of various Hunters. Today's assistant was Celvin. Ella thought he was almost as infuriating as Oliver, but not quite. If she had ever had a little brother, she was pretty sure he would have behaved exactly like Celvin.

Celvin was actually a great fighter, and getting better all the time. In fact, Ella was grateful that lessons were over for the day. She was looking forward to sitting down and soaking up some of earth's healing energy after dinner.

"Bear's already got your ale," Megs said. She met Ella with a towel, so she could freshen up. "Dinner should be out soon."

"What did you order me?"

"Fish mix sandwich,"

"I'm so hungry. Thanks," said Ella.

After Ella cleaned up, she and Megs ascended Marilla's basement stairs where Ella was lovingly attacked by two little, squealing toe-heads. Oliver had arrived to meet her for dinner. Looking at Oliver, she still felt her heartbeat quicken the same way it had that Solstice day on the Fainde River Bridge. Ella scooped up her twin daughters, Blom and Sara. She led them to a knotty wood table in the back of the bar.

Oliver helped Ella train Hunters, too, when Gunnar could nanny for Sara and Blom. Soon after the second Shadow attack during which came about Ohghee's demise, Ella and Oliver stood atop the cliffs in the very spot where the fern flower grew for Ella that night. There, under a lily-clad trellis, Ella and Oliver were married. The royal family had attended the wedding, and immediately following, held a second celebratory ceremony in honor of Ella and Oliver. They formally thanked Oliver and Ella for their service to Alveland, and honored Ella for defeating Ohghee.

Ella felt such relief on that day when Emil and Oliver finally extended the crossed fist of respect to each other. When they did, great clouds of gray emptied from their bodies and dissipated in the air. It only had taken twenty-seven years, but they finally got over their argument over the rope swing.

"M'Ma and P'Pa! Please, Ma, can we go?" Blom had just spotted Maria and Argon Marina at a corner table. Despite Ella's pressing desire to sit and rest, she brought the girls over to greet their grandee-elves.

"You watch them, Ma, while I go order food for the lasses, yes?" Ella asked.

Her mother happily obliged. She loved to tell Ella, Sara and Blom that Alveland's greatest calling in her life was being a grandee-elf.

"Bear, can I have two skyr and preserves plates for Sara and Blom?" Ella asked.

"Of course, Lady Ella," Bear said.

When Ella had given birth to her twin girls, King Frederick and Queen Sophia had bestowed the royal title on her, once again, in honor of Princess Kari. Ella had just gotten used to being plain, Miss Ella, that it felt strange all over again to be called 'Lady'.

"Oh, and two candy ales?"

Bear nodded.

When Ella returned to her table, Oliver and Mr Marina were pushing their tables together so the whole family could eat together. Oliver pulled a chair out for Ella, but as she sat down, Gunnar burst in on his hoverboard and took her chair.

"Hey!" said Ella.

"I just want to say hi to the lasses." Gunnar didn't even look at Ella when he spoke. He was already making faces at Sara and Blom.

"Give us a shimmer poppy!" Sara said.

Blom grabbed Gunnar's arm, already looking for the charmed flowers.

"What makes you think I have shimmer poppies?" Gunnar showed his empty hands.

Sara and Blom's faces fell.

"You always have shimmer poppies," Sara said.

"And if I did have a shimmer poppy, what makes you think I'd have two?" said Gunnar.

Sara and Blom looked hopeful. Gunnar reached into the hood of his elvish cloak and pulled out two purple poppies, charmed to look like they were reflecting the sun. Sara and Blom ran to the window of Marilla's to inspect the flowers in the light. Ella and Oliver greeted Gunnar who quickly left on his hoverboard. Ella was proud of Gunnar's transformation. He had begun to fight in Marilla's and hoped to attend Hunter University when he was old enough.

When he finally left, Ella collapsed in the chair.

Gunnar had asked her one day if the Shadow was gone forever. She knew it wasn't. Klayden and Burvanyek were still alive and controlling it. But she was a Huntress now, and she planned to stay that way. She would fight the Shadow and train others to do so as well. Oliver had already led a mission to the Far Lands. He used Dagur's map to locate another fortress of the Missing and set them free. The Hunters had a purpose and a plan, at least for the near future.

"Did anyone beat you in fighting today, Lady Ella?" Oliver asked. His gaze was still brooding as he sat down at the table across from her, but Ella knew the love which lurked behind his menacing expression.

"Of course not," Ella said.

"Then I better challenge you to a match," Oliver said. "It's a good thing I'm here."

Ella whined.

Bear showed up with a tray of food for the family.

"Thank the Spirits," Ella said. "We can't fight. The food has arrived."

"We'll consider it a forfeit, then," said Oliver.

Ella scowled.

"Are you going to accept that, Lady Ella?" Megs asked.

Ella straightened her linen pants and wrapped her long tresses up in a knot at the top of her head. There was no way Oliver was expecting her to forfeit. He knew her better than that. They both knew there would be a match between them, but a Lady needed her dinner first.

"Of course not," Ella said again. "I never do."

Printed in the USA
CPSIA information can be obtained
at www.ICGtesting.com
CBHW030314160724
11656CB00007B/315